"Can I at least come in and try to convince you?"

At her words, Cole turned. She was a shadow behind the screen door, a disembodied voice. "There's nothing you can say that will change my mind, but you can come inside and waste your breath if you want to."

Without waiting to see what she did, he made his way to the kitchen. Opening the refrigerator, he heard the door creak, followed by the sound of her boots on the floor. Grabbing two beers, he walked back to the den and handed her one of them.

"I want to go back," Taylor said softly. "I have to."

Despite himself, he asked, "Why?"

"I've never said goodbye. It's time for me to move on with my life, and I can't do that without going back to the…to the place it happened."

"Time to move on…" Her choice of words intrigued him. *She* was the one who'd left. He'd stayed. Every day he drove by the entrance to her ranch. Every day he led strangers into the land surrounding it. Every day he dealt with the pain in his hip.

She'd continued to speak, completely unaware of his thoughts. "Surely we could get to the canyon in a morning's ride? We could spend the night there, then—"

He stood. "I'm sorry, Taylor, but the answer's still no. I lost nothing out there that I need." His hands curled into fists at his sides. "You're on your own if you want to go back to Diablo."

Dear Reader,

No matter how far away I live, work or travel, Texas will always be my home, in my heart if nowhere else. As a child I grew up on the beaches of the Gulf of Mexico and as an adult I've lived all over the state. Whenever I'm gone, I look forward to returning, because Texas is incredibly unique and beautiful with a diversity of culture and land that can be found nowhere else.

This book reflects my love for one part of Texas—the wild empty reaches of the western half of the state. Lonely and vast, this area is very different from the tropical greenness of the Gulf Coast region or the flat terrain of the north. West Texas stretches past where the eye can see and goes on from there. The isolation and emptiness is almost impossible to describe. The sky's too blue, the air too sharp. My parents once owned a large ranch similar to the one in this book, and whenever I visited, I was torn between being afraid of its remoteness and enjoying the sensation of being the last person on earth.

Naturally, the people who inhabit this area are as unique as the land. They're independent, solitary creatures who like their space and want plenty of it. In this story, the love my characters share for the land is rivaled only by the passions they feel for each other. I hope you enjoy it.

Sincerely,

Kay David

THE MAN FROM HIGH MOUNTAIN
Kay David

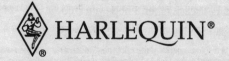

HARLEQUIN®

TORONTO • NEW YORK • LONDON
AMSTERDAM • PARIS • SYDNEY • HAMBURG
STOCKHOLM • ATHENS • TOKYO • MILAN • MADRID
PRAGUE • WARSAW • BUDAPEST • AUCKLAND

ISBN 0-373-70848-3

THE MAN FROM HIGH MOUNTAIN

Copyright © 1999 by Carla Luan.

This edition published by arrangement with Harlequin Books S.A.

Visit us at www.romance.net

Printed in U.S.A.

THE MAN FROM HIGH MOUNTAIN

CHAPTER ONE

TWICE A DAY THE DOCTOR came by her room. He was an old man, a country doctor, with a monk's fringe of hair around his head. His hands were gentle as they probed her bandages, especially the large, tight one holding her arm securely against her chest. On the third day, Taylor Matthews realized there was more in his eyes than concern. Through a still-lifting fog of painkillers and relaxants she finally recognized what it was late that afternoon.

His bright blue gaze held pity.

She turned her face away so he wouldn't see her tears, but he'd seen everything already and knew exactly what she was doing. When he finished changing all her dressings, he rested his hand against her shoulder, his touch cool against her skin.

"I'm so sorry, Mrs. Matthews." His voice was surprisingly deep. It echoed against the bare walls of the tiny West Texas hospital. "If it's any consolation, your husband died very quickly. The round went right through his heart. I doubt he felt a thing."

She moved her head against the pillow, squeezing her eyes tighter, her hair whispering against the crisp linens. From behind her eyelids, a burst of bright light accompanied the movement along with a stab of sudden sharpness. She welcomed the pain—it took her mind off everything else. She felt the pin-prick a moment later, and welcomed it, too. Blessed oblivion.

Just before she went back to sleep, someone came into the room and sat down. His step was odd, out of sync somehow, as if he too was wounded and here for care. Her eyelids were too heavy now to lift, but she didn't have to see the person to sense his presence. It spread over her room and filled the corners with a quiet and calming awareness. The sensation was comforting, almost as if she knew it was all right to go to sleep now because she wasn't alone anymore. He would stand watch over her. She was safe.

She drifted off, but the memories went with her.

THE DAY HAD BEEN WARM for fall, the West Texas sun so close to their heads Taylor had thought she could reach up and touch it. Climbing out of the ancient pickup, she'd gazed over the dusty barren landscape with dismay, half wondering, with affec-tion of course, if Jack had finally lost his mind.

She'd never seen a place so lonely and desolate.

"What do you think, hon?" Her husband of ten years, Jack Matthews, stood beside her like a child on Christmas Eve, waiting for her to open his pres-ent. Impatiently, he gave her his own opinion before she could answer him. "Isn't it great?" He held out his hands. "And look at that view! You can see for miles—and everything you see, we own!"

She turned then to look at him. His dark blue eyes, eyes she'd loved for so long, were staring into the distance, but she knew he wasn't seeing the enormous ranch he'd just bought. He was seeing the succession of mobile homes and dirty apartments and temporary shelters he and his brothers had lived in as children. He was seeing the hard life and the missed opportunities and the mother buried at the county's expense. He was seeing how far he'd come—from being a kid who owned one shirt to being a successful businessman who had now fulfilled his final dream. Owning a three-section ranch flat in the middle of West Texas. One thousand, nine hundred and twenty acres to be exact.

She swallowed the words she'd been about to say and put her arm around his shoulder. "It's beautiful, sweetheart. Truly gorgeous. I love it!"

He turned to her, his eyes sparkling. "Do you really?

"I do," she insisted loyally, nodding her head up and down. "It's absolutely perfect. Ranch heaven. I couldn't have picked a better place myself!"

Reassured by her words, as she knew he would be, he stepped away from the truck, the gravel beneath his boots crunching in the total and absolute isolation. The silence around them was overwhelming. Twenty miles off the main highway, they'd come at least fifty miles beyond that from the nearest town, High Mountain—which was, in fact, little more than a general store, a sad motel, and one lone Mexican food diner.

She glanced uneasily toward the guide at the rear of the truck. She hoped he was as good as he was supposed to be. What if they got lost? What if someone got hurt? They could be out here for days and see no one, absolutely no one. She studied the tall, slim man, understanding now that their lives literally depended on him.

He hadn't said two words to her after their introduction, but Jack had been totally at ease with Cole Reynolds. Usually cautious around strangers, Jack had been impressed with the taciturn man, telling Taylor last night that Cole knew the area better than anyone around. He was part Jumano Indian, Jack had explained, and had lived in the area all his life. Chattering about the details as they'd gotten ready for bed, Jack had seemed to enjoy the fact that their ranch was so huge they needed a tracker to lead them in.

"Once we get the roads paved, we'll be fine," he'd said, slipping between the covers, "but until then it's best if we let Cole help us. He's terrific— we definitely won't get lost with him in charge."

She walked to the back of the truck where the guide was unloading supplies. She paused by the bumper. "Need some help?"

At her voice, Cole Reynolds glanced up and met Taylor's gaze. She told herself she was being silly, but looking into his endlessly dark stare was like peering into a bottomless pit, and something tripped over her nerves. His eyes were so black she saw nothing except her own reflection. Suddenly rattled, she shifted her gaze. The skin that was stretched over his high cheekbones and bladelike nose was burnished into a deep rich tan. The dark hair that curled around the planes of his face only served to emphasize the copper tones.

"I'd like to do something," she said, repeating her offer just to break the tension she felt under his silent gaze. "May I help?"

"No thanks," he said curtly. Reaching back into the truck, he pulled out another pack, the muscles of his back straining beneath the white T-shirt he wore, the faded denim of his jeans stretching across his buttocks. He straightened. "You're gonna have enough to do once we start walking. You'd better wait in the shade by the truck for now. Conserve your energy."

His answer made perfect sense, and there was no hint of condescension in his voice. He was quietly competent and interested only in doing his job. Still, Taylor felt herself react. She had a sixth sense about people and something told her there was more to this man than the calm, cool exterior she saw. She wondered nervously what it was.

"What's wrong, Mr. Reynolds?" She spoke lightly, making her voice hold amusement. "Think I can't make it?"

The guide continued to pull gear out of the truck. After a moment he stopped and straightened completely. She hadn't realized how tall he was until then. Six feet plus, she figured.

"I think you're from Houston, I think you're not accustomed to this kind of heat, and I think you're in for a shock about just how rugged this part of Texas is." He stared at her a second longer, then reached into the back of the truck for a beat-up black cowboy hat. Tugging at it, one hand in the front, one in the rear, he settled it onto his head. "That's what I think."

She didn't quite know what to make of his answer. "Well, if that's the case, why did you agree to bring us out here?"

"It's what I do." The soft words, spoken in his West Texas drawl, hovered in the air between them. "I take people places they can't get to on their own. Then I bring them back."

"Are you two ready?" Jack appeared suddenly at Taylor's side, rubbed his hands and grinned engagingly. "I am. Can't wait as a matter of fact."

Grateful for the interruption, Taylor turned to her husband and smiled. "Think you'll feel that way tomorrow?"

He leaned over and kissed her on the nose. "No. By then, I'll want a hot bath and a pitcher of margaritas. But right now, I'm ready to see my ranch."

They spent the next half hour strapping on their backpacks and getting ready, Cole explaining the terrain they'd be crossing and what to watch for, including rattlesnakes. They had a lot of ground to cover. There was a deep water spring in the southwest corner and Jack wanted to check on the old ranch house that was supposed to be somewhere near the western edge, too. They set out, Taylor quickly forgetting about the man leading them as her husband eagerly began to show her his "spread," as he laughingly called the ranch.

By noon, though, Taylor's feet were screaming and she was a nervous wreck from imagining snakes under every rock. Just as she was about to give in and request a stop, Cole raised a hand and pointed to an outcrop of rocks ahead of them in the distance.

"That's the edge of the canyon. We'll stop there and eat lunch. Rest for a bit." He turned around and glanced at Taylor. His voice was noncommittal. "Okay with you, Miz Matthews?"

She answered breezily. "Whatever…"

He nodded once and continued to walk, the picture of competence. Something about him bothered her, but he definitely knew what he was doing, she had to admit that. Jack was right—they wouldn't get lost with Cole Reynolds in charge.

They reached the rocks within minutes. As she peeled off her pack, Jack came to her side. "Walk over to the canyon with me," he said. Glancing at Cole who was preparing their lunch, Jack smiled, the expression lifting his mouth and crinkling the corners of his eyes. "I want to show it to you by myself."

She forgot about her feet as she saw the enthusiasm in his expression. A surge of love came over her, and she took her husband's hand. "I'd like that."

She'd expected something different, but the sight that greeted them when they reached the edge stole Taylor's breath. As if a giant had taken a hatchet and chopped open the earth, a red slash, at least a hundred feet wide, gaped at their feet, going on for miles and miles. The gorge was deep, too, so deep even the noontime sun didn't dispel the shadows in the bottom. In the eerie silence she could hear the faint sound of rushing water at the bottom and a jingling sound, almost like a horse's halter. They edged closer until they were standing right on the rim, on one of the rocky ledges surrounding the very perimeter. Taylor felt dizzy.

Jack pointed downward. "That's the Rio Diablo. The ranch got its name from the river. El Rancho del Diablo—The Devil's Ranch." Tilting his head to indicate the land on the other side, he spoke again. "And that's Mexico."

"It's beautiful." Looking around the stark and lonely landscape, Taylor realized for the first time she meant what she'd just said. The land *was* beautiful. Bleak and barren, it stretched on forever, the red rocks and few gnarled trees standing out starkly against a sky that particular shade of blue that burned into your eyes when you stared at it. The quiet was thick enough to taste, and the air so thin it carried sound like a ribbon of silk in the wind. Overhead a hawk circled lazily, his cries piercing.

Taylor had become a determined city girl after growing up in Montana, but there was something about Diablo. It was unexpectedly exhilarating, even though it was intimidating, too.

She turned to Jack to say so. To tell him she loved him and how happy she was he'd bought this present for himself, this ranch that represented so much.

And that's when the first shot rang out.

For just a moment, she was puzzled. The noise was foreign to her, abrupt and scary, disturbing the silence unexpectedly and not making sense. Staring at Jack, she frowned and started to ask him what it was—then the second shot sounded and a sudden bloom of red appeared on her shoulder, the one next to Jack's. She looked at her shirt with a baffled expression, then comprehension came. And with it, pain.

"My God," she said, wonder filling her voice. "I—I think I've been shot."

Another crack broke the silence, this one zinging past her ear. Taylor screamed then, and Jack threw himself in front of her, his frantic hands on her shoulders pulling her toward the ground, realizing a second too late the direction from which the shots were coming. "Get down," he yelled. "Get down!"

Before they could move, the gun sounded again. His body in front of hers, Jack pitched forward, a searing pain exploding in Taylor's shoulder at the very same moment—one bullet hitting him then her. She cried out and staggered as Jack's fingers curled painfully into her arms, his sudden weight coming against her and dragging them both into the red dust. She tasted it, like blood, on her tongue.

"Jack!" Refusing to see the mingling blood and the emptiness coming into her husband's eyes, she screamed his name again. "Jack! My God, Jack!"

Fading fast, he looked into her eyes. "I love you," he whispered.

COLE WAS BESIDE TAYLOR within seconds. Kneeling, he said nothing, but moved fast. Rolling Jack off her, he took a handful of Taylor's collar and yanked her back and up, away from the edge of the canyon.

"No!" Struggling against the blackness that threatened to overcome her, she cried out. "Stop...stop! We have to get Jack."

"You're hurt. I have to get you out." Cole's voice was ragged, panting.

She fought him, kicking at his legs and pounding his chest with her fists, a flash of pain ricocheting off her arm and slicing down the rest of her body. "No," she screamed again. "I want Jack. Jack—"

Cole ignored her cries. Slipping his arms beneath her own, he scooped her up and began to run.

The fifth shot got him.

With a grunt of pain, he fell heavily, Taylor going down with him. He was moving again within seconds, scrambling backward through the dust and scrubby cactus. Taylor continued to fight him, sobbing as she shrieked, a fiery pain fueling her grief and confusion and anger.

They reached a half-dead mesquite tree, and dragging her into the scant protection it offered, Cole finally stopped. Groggy and growing weak, Taylor had only one thought: She had to get to Jack. On her hands and knees, crying and wounded, she reached out and grasped one of the rough branches of the mesquite. The rough bark bit into her skin, scraping it raw. Ignoring this new pain, she used the limb to pull herself upright and staggered out into the open, taking two steps back the way they'd come.

A final shot rang out.

SHE CAME TO BRIEFLY. Someone was standing beside the bed, someone tall. She forced her eyes open as he touched her hand. Dark eyes met hers, then her eyelids fluttered down again. Before she went completely under, details, like passing headlights, flashed into her mind. An endless, agonizing ride to the hospital with an empty seat beside her. The doctors and nurses murmuring quietly. Pain, pain that made black dots dance in front of her eyes and buzzing noises sound in her ears. And finally the terrible, terrible knowledge coming to her that her life, as it had been, was over.

Her husband was dead.

CHAPTER TWO

Two years later—Houston, Texas

"YOU'VE COME TO MEAN the world to me, Taylor. And I want everyone to know it."

Taylor Matthews lifted her champagne glass to her lips and looked over the rim at Richard Williams. They were sitting in a booth at Tony's, the most expensive restaurant in town, and Richard fit in very well with the crowd around them. Black suit, gold watch, silver hair. He was sixteen years older than Taylor, but in excellent physical shape, a strong handsome man. He exercised a lot—ran and played squash five times a week—and was proud of how he looked. Jack's partner in the art gallery they'd owned together, Richard had also been Taylor's rock since his death. He reached across the table and put his hand over her fingers, squeezing gently. Between them, resting on the table in a black velvet box, a four-carat marquise diamond ring winked and flashed in the candlelight.

"I know these last few years have been hard for you, darling, but I can make that better. Let's take this final step and commit to each other. I think you'd be so happy, you'd forget all about the past.''

Taylor smiled gently. He was a sweetheart, but Richard didn't really understand. When Jack had died that hot summer day two years ago, Taylor's life had been changed forever. For a long time, things other people took for granted were beyond her reach. Things like sleeping through the night. Eating with appetite. Making love... Each and every day Taylor had struggled, one way or another. Richard had helped tremendously, but she would never forget what had happened.

She couldn't. Deep down inside her a huge, gaping hole existed that would never be filled. Dr. Kornfeld, her therapist, had assured her it wouldn't always be that way, but Taylor knew better. While some days were better than others, the truth was, her mental well-being had suffered greatly, and it had been getting even worse recently, her nerves a mess, her emotions upside down. The nightmares, always bad since that day, had gotten inexplicably more severe the past few months. Every night disturbing images of blood and dust, screams and fear, were tangling her in the sheets and bringing her to abrupt awareness. She kept hearing the local sheriff's voice in her mind, describing Jack's killers.

"Druggers. Probably crossing the river with a load. Thought you might see 'em and report it. Easier to shoot ya." A shake of the head. "We'll never find 'em. Gone into the mountains, already in Mexico. Too late…too late.''

Jack's murder had gone unpunished and the fairness and principles he'd believed in had gone by the wayside. He'd never received the kind of justice he'd deserved. She mentally shook herself and pulled away from the images and haunting voice to concentrate on the present. After Jack's death, Richard had guided her through all the legal problems and had virtually run the business single-handedly. Slowly, so slowly she hadn't even noticed until the past year, their relationship had evolved into something else, in spite of her continued emotional problems. Richard had turned into more than a friend.

But an engagement? Was she ready for that step?

She looked across the table at the handsome, elegant man. What she felt for him wasn't the wild, at-first-sight-and-forever kind of love she'd had with Jack, but a woman could only hope to be that lucky once in a lifetime, and she'd had her turn. Which, actually, was a perfectly acceptable situation to Taylor. She didn't even *want* that kind of connection again—it hurt too much when it ended.

Richard lifted her hand to his lips and brushed his mouth over the tips of her fingers. ''What do you say?'' He nodded toward the diamond ring and smiled. ''Do you think that might be your size?''

She answered his smile with one of her own, but deep down, more questions began to assail her. Was it fair to Richard to commit to a relationship if she wasn't sure?

As if sensing her hesitation, he pressed. "I don't want to wait any longer, Taylor. I know my feelings for you are stronger than yours are for me, but with time, that will change, I'm sure of it. You'll grow to love me just as much as I love you."

His words made her feel instantly guilty and unappreciative of everything he'd done for her. She tried to explain. "Richard, you've been so kind, so patient, and I really do appreciate it, but I…I'm having nightmares again…and well…I'm not sure I'm ready yet. I want to sell the ranch—"

He picked up the box holding the diamond and took her hand in his, interrupting her words to slip the ring over her finger. "Maybe this could help make up your mind."

She looked at the enormous diamond. It felt heavy and foreign on her finger and had obviously cost a fortune. "It's really beautiful but—"

"No more buts. I picked it out just for you. Please…"

She hesitated again, then spoke softly. "Richard…I—I can't do anything until I take care of the ranch first. You know that. We've discussed this before."

He shook his head slowly, a look of patience on his aristocratic features. "Please don't be offended, but I think you're using that as an excuse, sweetheart. It's time for our relationship to get serious. It's time to move on.''

''And selling the ranch is the first step to doing that.'' She leaned across the table. ''Don't you see, Richard? The only closure I'll be able to find with Jack's death will be gained by getting rid of Diablo. His killers got away, but I can get rid of the place if nothing else.'' She leaned back in her chair. ''Besides, there's no reason on earth to keep the property—''

''Darling, there's lots of reasons. That land is gorgeous, for one! When I saw it—that time I went out with Jack before he bought it—I loved the place. Anyone would. And if land prices keep going up, it's going to be worth a fortune some day. If you hang on to the ranch, you could end up being a very rich woman.'' He smiled again. ''That's what I'd call a good reason to keep it.''

''I'm rich already,'' she said bluntly. ''Jack left an insurance policy of almost a million dollars. Between that and the business, I'll never need any money.'' Without thinking, she began to knead her shoulder. Beneath the silk, she could feel the slight indentation of the scar. Of the bullet wound. ''What I don't need is that land. The memories are too bad, and I want to get rid of it. I could never go back there.''

''Then don't go. But don't sell it.''

''I have to.''

''You're being foolish.''

"I don't care."

They stared at each other, a standoff in the making. He was being practical, realistic, the way men usually were. She was going beyond that, into an emotional abyss he didn't understand and she couldn't really explain.

A moment's silence passed, then Richard reached for the champagne bottle and refilled her flute. "What do you say we talk about this later? I want this to be our special night." The pale gold wine bubbled up and edged over the rim of the glass, dampening the tablecloth. Richard's eyes met hers above the candles. "Let's just celebrate, then if you really do want to sell the place, we'll discuss it some more, I promise."

They'd already discussed the issue more than once, and each time he'd tried to change her mind. In fact, now that she thought about it, she was sure that's why her nightmares had returned. She'd felt compelled to press the issue more and more lately, maybe because she'd sensed Richard's proposal was coming and knew she couldn't decide with the ranch hanging over her. For a second, she considered persevering. Then after a moment more of thought, Taylor gave in. He was right. This wasn't the time or the place.

"All right," she said quietly. "We'll talk about it later. But in the meantime, you keep the ring."

She tugged at the band of gold with the giant stone, but he reached across the table and stopped her a second time from taking it off. "No, please, Taylor. Wear it, look at the diamond, and think of me…and think how happy I could make you if you'd let me."

"But—"

"Please…"

She hesitated, then finally acquiesced. He'd done so much for her, had helped with everything. He'd be the perfect husband, she was sure. "All right. But I'm not saying yes."

He grinned. "But you're not saying no."

She smiled back. "I promise you I'll think about it."

"Good." He opened his menu with an approving smile that told her he knew what her answer would be, then began to discuss what they should order. She listened inattentively, and her fingers found her shoulder and rubbed it slowly.

THE FOLLOWING WEEK came and went, and they didn't talk about selling the ranch. And the week after that, they didn't discuss it either. Always on the edge, Taylor felt the pendulum of her emotions swinging out of control, her nerves like wires, stripped and bare. She talked the situation over with Dr. Kornfeld, but Taylor seemed unable to control her thoughts. As if they had a mind of their own, they began to coalesce and focus with an intensity bordering on obsession. All she could think about was one thing—selling Diablo. If she just did that, she knew everything else would fall into place. Getting rid of the ranch and all the emotional baggage it carried would set her free. A telephone call to a real estate agent wouldn't do it, either. She didn't tell Richard, or Dr. Kornfeld, but the more Taylor thought about it, the more certain she became.

She had to go back, back to Diablo. To step in the red dust and to taste the fear before she could put it behind her and get on with her life.

"I'll be calling Martha next week about the first container, so be sure and have her talk to the shipper before then. Also we'll need to arrange for special storage. The French armoire Mrs. Rogers wants will need to be in a humidity-controlled place until we see how much restoration it requires." Richard looked over the edge of his glasses at Taylor. "You know where I'll be staying, don't you?"

They were at the gallery, tending to a few last-minute details before Richard left on a six-week buying trip to Europe. The trip had come up unexpectedly.

From the other side of the partner's desk they shared, Taylor answered, struggling to focus on his words and not her thoughts. "You always stay at the same place, Richard. If I need you, I'll be able to find you, don't worry."

He moved to her side with an apologetic smile. "I'm getting uptight, aren't I?"

"It's okay. Trips like this take a lot of coordination. I'd be uptight, too."

"I'm glad you understand." He reached out and smoothed her hair. "I want you to promise me something, though."

She looked up. "What?"

"I want you to take some time off while I'm gone. The gallery will be just fine with both of us gone. Martha can handle any crisis better than even you or I, so I want you to relax a little. Go down to the beach house or even better, fly to Florida for a week or so. You need some time off—to think about our future together."

He was always so generous, so kind. Why did she have to spoil it all by insisting they talk about the ranch? Taylor took a deep breath and started to speak, but Richard had already turned and disappeared into the hall. He came back into the office a few moments later, a sheaf of invoices in his hand. A deep furrow of concern was drawn across his forehead as he studied them, and when he laid them down on the desk, he sighed so heavily she had to put aside her thoughts of Diablo.

"What's wrong?"

"I wanted to take a quick look at last month's statements before I left and they're as bad as I thought. We've got to start doing better. Our profits are slipping. We've had some good sales lately, but nothing spectacular." He took a peppermint from his pocket, unwrapped it and slipped the candy into his mouth. Absentmindedly, he twisted the tiny plastic sheath that had covered the candy into a double knot. He did this constantly. She found the wrappers everywhere. "Maybe I can find something in London to tempt Mr. Metzner. That would help."

"But we're doing fine." Taylor was puzzled. She did the bookkeeping. She knew their bottom line down to the penny.

"I want to do better than fine, Taylor," he answered with a hint of irritation. "The space next door is going to be available in a month or so and I really wanted it—so we can expand."

Richard's only fault was his ambition—sometimes it took him too far. Jack had told her about some of the acquisitions he'd made sight unseen. The expenditures had frightened Jack, a more conservative businessman, but in the end they'd turned out to be extremely profitable, thank God.

She spoke uneasily. "You didn't sign anything, did you? Like a lease or something?" Beneath the desk, she tangled her fingers nervously.

"Of course not," he answered patiently. "You know I'd discuss something like that with you first."

"Well, I don't think we need to expand right now. We're doing very well as it is."

Martha Klein, their assistant, appeared at the door. "Your tickets just arrived, Richard. And the driver's here to take you to the airport. Are you ready?"

Taylor stared at the woman with dismay. "He's early—"

"Tell him I'll be right there, Martha." Looking back at Taylor, Richard held out his hands, a sudden expression of contrition on his handsome features. "Look—I'm sorry, sweetheart, we *are* doing wonderfully, but you know me. I just get carried away sometimes. I want the best for you—for us. That's all. You understand, don't you?"

Taylor nodded. "I do, but—"

The office door opened again. Martha peeked inside. "Are these all of your bags out here? Nothing else?"

"That's it."

Taylor's shoulders dropped. There was no more time—she couldn't bring up the ranch issue now. How could they resolve it like this, here, in the next two minutes?

Richard misinterpreted her movement. "C'mon, darling. I won't be gone that long. Chin up." He held out his arms and she stepped into them. For a moment, they hugged, then Richard released her, kissing her on the cheek. "Take care of yourself," he instructed, "and think about how much I love you. That's the only important thing."

Taylor stared at the door as it closed softly behind him. A few minutes later, she heard the limo pull out of the driveway. Turning in her office chair, she stared out the window at the fall mums lining the walkway into the gallery. They were orange and gold and red, and their colors made her think of a different place and time. In her mind, she saw a dusty, barren landscape, a tall, dark stranger, and a crimson stain that spread much too fast. Unconsciously, she raised her right hand toward her left shoulder, but before her fingers found their mark, she dropped her hand to the top of the desk. She thought for a very long time, then reached for the phone.

CHAPTER THREE

TAYLOR SNAPPED HER weekender shut and took one last look around her bedroom. She planned on being gone no more than a few days. The real estate agent had told her he could have the papers drawn up during that time, and it wouldn't take more than an hour to sign them all afterward. A power of attorney was a simple thing to execute. When a buyer for the ranch was found, she wouldn't have to return.

Selling the ranch without Richard's approval was not the best way to demonstrate her level of commitment to him but she didn't really have a choice. Without taking care of this detail first, there wouldn't be a relationship, much less an engagement. She couldn't explain all her feelings to Richard, but in time, he'd understand. He was a patient, caring man and he'd see her point.

FIVE HOURS LATER Taylor stood at the rental car counter in Meader, the nearest town of any size to High Mountain. The place was barely bigger than High Mountain but it did have a small regional airport. Most of its customers were oil field workers who serviced the wells that dotted the lonely countryside. Taylor took the first vehicle the clerk mentioned, a black Blazer, and was on the road quickly. Two hundred miles stretched between Meader and High Mountain with few places to stop in between. She wanted to get as many of those miles behind her before dark as she could.

But night came almost without warning. One minute there was light on the highway and the next, it was gone. Taylor felt swallowed by the darkness. She glanced down at her watch and saw with shock three hours had passed, and she hadn't even been aware where she was or what was happening. The Blazer sped through the ghostly quiet, following the ribbon of highway, its beams cutting into the shadows. She realized, too, the terrain had changed, and she hadn't noticed, switching from planted fields and oil wells to rockier ground, too rough to support much more than the sturdy-looking cattle the lights occasionally caught near a fence line. By the time she rolled into High Mountain, a half hour later, even that had changed. There was nothing but scrub and dust and cactus beyond the faded sign announcing the town limits.

Pulling in to the only motel, Taylor parked the truck and shut it off. With a weary sigh she momentarily rested her head on the steering wheel, her back throbbing with the strain of sitting first in the plane and then in the vehicle for so long. The shooting had left its mark on her in a lot of different ways, but one painful reminder was a nagging backache if she didn't stretch and move around frequently. After a moment's uneasy rest, she opened the door and slowly stepped out into the darkness.

The air was cool and biting, a pleasant surprise after Houston, especially when she breathed deeply and realized it carried a hint of cedar and wood smoke. Somewhere in the distance, a dog howled.

She made her way to the office of the motel. A sleepy clerk, his name tag crooked, his face confused, answered the buzzer and ten minutes later, Taylor had a room. Worn and less than fashionable, it was at least clean. Closing the curtains, she stripped, showered and fell into bed.

She was too tired to even dream.

COLE REYNOLDS HEARD the truck approaching long before he saw it. He was sitting on his porch cleaning his rifle and the mountain air brought the engine's whine to his ears a full twenty seconds before his eyes found the telltale cloud of dust marking the vehicle's progress. By the time the black Blazer pulled up into his yard, Cole had the .30-06 reassembled and tucked behind his rocking chair, no trace of it or the cleaning materials anywhere in sight.

He waited patiently to see who emerged from the unfamiliar vehicle. He didn't recognize the Blazer, and its darkened windows gave him no hint. Whoever was behind the wheel was looking for him, though, of that he was sure. No one drove this far without knowing he was at the end of the road.

The door slowly opened. He caught a glimpse of blond hair and one stretched-out leg—long and slim—then the driver rounded the truck and came toward him. He hadn't seen the woman in two years and the last time he had, she'd been covered in bandages and bruises. But he would have recognized Taylor Matthews anywhere.

His chest tightened, and he found himself gripping the arms of the rocker, a low, dull pain throbbing in his hip and resonating upwards. Ignoring the sensation, as he always did, he pushed himself up. By the time she reached the bottom step, he was staring down at her.

She looked as good as he remembered. Glittery and golden and polished, like the pebbles he sometimes found near the Rio Diablo. *Fool's Gold,* he reminded himself.

He spoke pleasantly, hiding all his reactions. "Miz Matthews—what a surprise. What's brought you back to this part of the world?"

She stood in a pool of sunshine, her green eyes taking in his house, his truck to one side, even his dog lying on the rug by the front door before she spoke. "I've decided to sell the ranch."

Her answer was as direct as his question. No niceties, no preliminaries, no small talk. He started to reply, but she spoke again. "Before I sell, I want to go out one more time. To the...to the place it happened. Will you take me?''

If she'd walked up on the porch and punched him in the stomach, he wouldn't have lost his breath any faster. For a single long moment, he stared at her, the midday warmth rising between them, a fly buzzing against the screen door, then he spoke. ''No.''

He turned around and walked slowly to his door. Before he could open it, she spoke from behind him.

''That's it? Just no?''

He didn't bother to turn around. ''That's it,'' he answered. ''Just no.'' Opening the screen door, he stepped inside the cabin. The sudden dimness was such a change from the outside, he blinked, his vision going dark for just a second. By the time it returned, her steps were sounding on the wooden porch and she was speaking to him through the screen.

''Can I at least come in and try to convince you?''

He turned then, slowly, almost awkwardly. She was a shadow behind the screen, a disembodied voice. ''There's nothing you could say that would change my mind, but you can come inside and waste your breath if you want to.''

Without waiting to see what she did, he made his way to the small kitchen tucked in one corner of the house. Opening the refrigerator, he heard the screen door creak, followed by the sound of her boots on the floor. He didn't look back. ''Beer?'' he called out.

"That'd be nice," she answered.

Taking two Coronas from the refrigerator, he opened them both, then walked back to the den and over to the desk where she was standing. He handed her one of the cold, clear bottles, then brought his own to his mouth. When he lowered it, the beer was all but gone.

In the dimness, her green eyes glowed.

"I want to go back," she said softly. "I have to."

Despite himself, he asked, "Why?"

She hesitated for only a moment. "I've never turned loose of it. Never said goodbye. It's time for me to move on with my life, and I can't seem to do that without taking care of this first."

"Time to move on..." Her choice of words intrigued him. *She* was the one who'd fled. He'd stayed. Every day he drove by the entrance to her ranch. Every day he led strangers into the land surrounding it. Every day he dealt with the ragged pain in his hip.

"Richard Williams—my husband's partner—has asked me to marry him," she said. As if that explained everything. "I promised him I'd...think about it but I had to come out here first."

He saw it now—the wink of an enormous diamond on her left hand. She'd worn a plain gold band before. Funny how he remembered that, but he could see the ring as if it'd been yesterday—those pale, long fingers lying on the white sheets of the hospital bed, the gold glinting dully. It'd felt cold against his own hand when he'd covered her fingers with his.

"Congratulations," he said.

She looked startled by his answer, her eyes rounding for an instant before she shuttered her expression. "Thank you."

He turned around and sat down heavily in the old recliner beside the couch. She continued to stand by the desk.

He spoke to break the silence, his voice was raspy in the quiet. "How you feeling? Everything heal okay?"

He watched as her fingers went to her upper arm. It was an unconscious movement, he was sure, because she merely touched her shoulder then dropped her hand back to her side. "I went through a lot of physical therapy," she answered. "It was...hard."

The word seemed unsatisfying to her. She pursed her lips and stared at him, then spoke again, this time telling him the truth because they were both survivors and he'd understand. "Actually, it hurt like hell. I didn't think I'd make it."

He nodded. Nothing else was necessary.

She sat down on the couch, the springs protesting her weight. "Why won't you take me?"

He drained his beer and set the bottle on the floor beside the chair. The decision to lie to her was an easy one because it wouldn't have been a lie a few months before. And for a lesser man, it would still be the truth. Doc Watts had hidden his surprise, but to Cole his recovery hadn't been unexpected. He'd simply willed his hip to work again, had not accepted the unacceptable. He'd tortured himself into health, walking the mountains till he'd dropped, carving a place deep inside him for the pain and not letting it out.

He met her eyes without flinching. "I can't. The terrain's too rough for my hip."

Her breath caught in her chest. He could see her sudden stillness.

"Your hip? What happened? You were okay when I left."

He hesitated, then spoke. "An infection developed. Doc Watts had to go back in and operate again. Things didn't turn out quite as great as he hoped."

"You don't track anymore? At all?"

He shook his head. "I didn't say that."

"Then what do you mean?"

"I guide, but day trips only and by horseback, not on foot."

"We drove most of the way, remember?"

His eyes met hers. "I remember every detail, Miz Matthews, believe me."

She stood up. Moving to the window at the back of the cabin, she spoke softly. "It's Taylor." She paused. "My first name is Taylor."

He said nothing. Outside, the heat shimmered in the distance. Finally she turned around.

"I—I had no idea…", Her hand fluttered toward his leg. "I'm sorry."

"It's not your fault. Your finger wasn't on the trigger."

"But you wouldn't have been shot if we hadn't hired you…if you hadn't tried to help me." A longer pause. "If I hadn't tried to go back for Jack."

"You didn't know."

"I'm sorry," she said again.

Their eyes met, something shining in the cool green depths of hers that he didn't want to see. He shrugged.

She bore the silence a moment longer, then she came to where he sat. "What if we took it easy? Drove in with horses, then camped for the night?" Her perfume reached out and curled around him. She was as beautiful as she had been two years ago. Just as beautiful and just as appealing. She had a delicate air about her, seemed even more fragile than she had been that first time they'd met. He imagined she wouldn't last long in the harsh West Texas environment.

She continued to speak, completely unaware of his thoughts. "Surely we could get to the canyon in a morning's ride, couldn't we? We could spend another night out, then—"

He pushed himself up from the chair. "I'm sorry, Miz Matthews—Taylor—but the answer's still no. I lost nothing out there I need." His hands curled into fists at his side, and he pulled his lips into one straight line. "You're on.your own if you want to go back to Diablo."

TAYLOR FOUND HERSELF walking down Main Street that afternoon with little else to do. Jim Henderson, the real estate agent, couldn't see her until later, and she'd planned on using this time to get ready for her trip out to the ranch.

Seeing the diner ahead, she realized she hadn't eaten since breakfast so she headed inside and ordered a small salad and a cup of coffee. She was the only patron in the tiny restaurant, and her meal came within seconds. Lifting her fork, she looked at the sad bowl of wilted lettuce and tomatoes, then sighed deeply and put the fork down.

Turning her head, she stared out the window beside her. In the distant background, the ragged tops of the Davis Mountains pulled her gaze, their uneven edges as sharp and treacherous as the look that had been in Cole Reynolds's dark eyes.

Deep down, a heavy tug of guilt pulled at her. Because of what had happened to them, Cole had been forced to change his way of life. Because of her and Jack. Because of some idiot with a gun. Taking a sip of coffee, she wondered suddenly how Cole had actually managed to get them both to the hospital. She'd never really asked anyone for the details. She'd been in too much pain to even care at first, and once she'd started to heal, she'd been overwhelmed by grief. As soon as Doc Watts had decided she could be moved, they'd flown her out, taken her directly to Houston and a rehab hospital. She'd never had a chance to say much more than "thanks," and in truth, she hadn't wanted to talk with Cole. Not then.

Staring into her coffee cup, she felt a flash of shameful embarrassment. The man had saved her life, and she hadn't even thanked him properly. All she'd done was show up on his doorstep and demand that he take her back to the one place he probably didn't want to see himself.

A practical thought brought her full circle, right and wrong aside. With Cole out of the question, she'd have to find another guide. She could probably drive as far as Cole's truck had, but after that, the situation would be hopeless. She didn't know which way the canyon was or even how to get there. Her eyes left the mountain top and settled back on Main Street. She hadn't come this far to go back now. Surely there were other guides in High Mountain. Other ways to get to Rancho Diablo.

TAYLOR BEGAN HER QUEST for another tracker the following day, but it became apparent almost immediately that she was out of luck.

She sat on her bed by the phone, her fingers resting on the receiver. She'd called everyone in town that she remotely knew and quite a few she didn't, and all their answers had been the same when she asked for a name. Cole Reynolds. He was the only guide in town. At least they had said *that,* she thought dejectedly. During the past twenty-four hours, the phone in her hotel room had rung six times and the caller had said nothing, absolutely nothing. She'd marched to the office after the third time to complain, but the clerk had insisted someone had been on the line asking for her room. Taylor had heard only silence.

By the end of the second day, just when she thought things couldn't get any worse, she walked out her door and then stopped abruptly, her mouth dropping open in amazement.

All four tires of the Blazer were flat.

Cursing her bad luck and the rental car agency, she quickly crossed the parking lot and bent down to stare dejectedly at the tires. She'd have to call a tow truck, then find the nearest tire store, if there even was one in High Mountain. Before she could finish the thought, a moment later, she realized the tires weren't merely flat.

They'd been slashed.

Stunned, she knelt by the back fender, her fingers going to the ribbons of rubber that hung loosely from each tire, her mouth turning as dry as the red dust at her feet. Why would someone do this? Why?

A cold shiver washed over her back as she stared at the tire. Whoever had done this had been angry. They could have just let the air out and accomplished the same thing. Instead, they'd completely destroyed the tires, even nicking the paint in one of the fenders, she noticed a second later.

She stood up resolutely and began to walk down the street toward the sheriff's office. She had come back to Diablo to get her life in order. Slashed tires and midnight calls weren't going to stop her.

HE TOLD HIMSELF it was no big deal.

Coming into town for his supplies—a full two days earlier than he usually did—meant nothing. Cole was *not* looking for Taylor Matthews and he didn't give a damn whether she made it out to Rancho Diablo or not. It was none of his business.

None of his business—just like the lights he sometimes saw down by the river and the muffled sound of horse hooves that often accompanied them. None of his business—just like the occasional gunfire he heard echoing down the canyon. None of it was his business.

But as he pulled his pickup truck into the last open spot on Main, Cole found himself looking around, his hands gripping the steering wheel. He knew she was still in town—half a dozen people had told him she was asking around for another guide. She was looking for trouble, he thought, just begging for it. His gaze went up the street then down. The black Blazer was nowhere in sight, and the tightness in his chest let up slightly.

Opening his door, he eased out of the vehicle and stepped down into the street with relief.

The feeling was short-lived.

He saw her almost immediately. She was inside Pearson's, the general store located directly in front of Cole's pickup, and a stack of camping gear was piled beside her. Through the shimmering plate glass window, Cole noted a sleeping bag, a camp stove, a backpack, and various other small packages and boxes. He swore under his breath. Unless she had developed some skills he didn't know about in the past two years, Taylor Matthews was about to do something incredibly stupid.

He didn't stop to think—he went directly inside the store and walked up to her. "What are you doing?"

Her eyes jerked to his. They were light green, the exact same color as the leaves of the cypress tree, the one that grew by the springs out at the ranch. "I'm taking a trip," she said slowly. "A camping trip."

"Where?"

"To Diablo."

"I don't think that's a very smart thing to do."

She tilted her head, the morning sunlight picking out reddish glints in her hair. "I'm a grown woman, Mr. Reynolds. I can take care of myself."

"Like you did two years ago?" Her eyes widened at the bluntness of his words, but he didn't back down. He couldn't. She had no business going out there alone. She was totally incapable of dealing with the land and its dangers. "I would think you'd know better by now."

Her cheeks flushed slightly. "I'm well aware of the risks, but I've found another way to accomplish my goals. A way that doesn't include you."

"And that would be?"

"With Charles Karnet."

"Karnet's a helicopter pilot, not a tracker."

"I know that. He's going to fly me into the ranch and drop me off by the canyon."

"And leave you alone?"

She nodded.

A nearby movement suddenly caught Cole's eye, and he turned his head to see Earl Pearson. Hovering near them, beside a stack of used paperbacks, the owner of the general store was listening to every word they said. The man was harmless, but Cole didn't like anyone hearing his business. He took Taylor's elbow and led her a few steps away. Beneath his fingers, her skin was smooth and cool. He dropped her arm as soon as he could.

"You're making a mistake. You shouldn't go out there."

Her expression became guarded, a shadow coming into her eyes he didn't quite understand. "What are you saying?"

He ignored her question. He wasn't sure he knew *how* to answer it. "Why do you want to go there so badly?"

"I explained that already," she said. "I need closure. I can't go forward until I put what happened behind me—''

"Can't you do that from here? Why would you want to go back to the place your husband died? The place that holds so much of your own blood?"

Her eyes turned a darker shade of green. Behind the color was pain. "You don't understand. If Jack had gotten some kind of justice, I might have put it to rest, but he never did. I've tried to forget about it, but I can't and it's getting worse. I can't sleep, I can't eat, I have nightmares—'' She stopped abruptly and took a very deep breath. "I have to go out there. I don't have a choice.''

Cole stared at her, his gut churning. The hell of it was—he *did* understand what she was saying. He understood perfectly. For some crazy reason, he'd had to visit Rancho Diablo as soon as he could after the shooting. It'd been pointless, though. The "closure" she sought wouldn't be discovered in the desolate stretches of the ranch any more than his had. The only difference between them was he knew it. She didn't.

He tried once more. He had to. "You shouldn't go out there by yourself.''

When she spoke, her voice was fierce. "Then come with me. Let me say my goodbyes the way I want to. After that, I'll never ask you to do anything for me. I'll leave here, and you'll never see me again. I promise.''

If he turned his back on her and she went alone,

she probably wouldn't return alive. If he got involved and they went together, God only knew what would happen. He'd been fighting off his memories for so long, the reality of actually being with her might be too much.

One way or the other, Cole was doomed.

He glanced outside to the mountains and wondered just what kind of mistake he was making. He was afraid he knew but there was nothing that could be done about it. He didn't have a choice, either. Gesturing toward the pile of camping equipment at her feet, he met her gaze once more. "Be at my place at five in the morning. We'll drive as far as we can, then pack in. Count on two days, one night." He paused. "And get rid of this junk. I've got everything we'll need."

Her emerald eyes turned warm all of a sudden. "Thank y—"

He stopped her, his callused palm held out between them. "Don't thank me for this, Taylor. Believe me, I'm not doing you any favors."

CHAPTER FOUR

SURPRISED BY COLE'S sudden capitulation but too happy to question it, Taylor watched him climb awkwardly into his beat-up truck a few seconds later. Through the window, she stared as he pulled away, red dust rising in a cloud thick enough to obscure his departure. When she turned around, the owner of the store was looking at her. He was a strange little man with a rounded face and eyes that didn't quite match. As she watched, the left one twitched violently.

"I'm afraid I won't be needing these things after all," she said apologetically. "My plans have changed."

The man tilted his head toward the street. "You going to Diablo with him?"

His question surprised her, but then she reminded herself that High Mountain wasn't Houston. Everyone knew everyone else. "Yes," she answered. "Cole will be guiding me in. He has his own equipment. You know who I am?"

He nodded. "Everybody knows who you are. We got long memories 'round here."

"Then I guess you know I'm selling the ranch."

His eyes narrowed, but the left one continued to twitch. "Sell Diablo?" He shook his head with a jerky rhythm that matched the movement in his eye. "That'll never happen."

"Why on earth would you say that? I'm sure someone will want it."

"Never. Leastways not anybody 'round here." He punched his lips out and shook his head. "Everybody in High Mountain knows that place is haunted."

Stunned into silence, all she could do was stare at the man.

"Sorry to be putting it that way to you, so blunt and everything, but it's the truth. Strange lights, weird sounds—you name it and it goes on out there. Was happening a long time before your husband even bought the place. He shoulda knowed better."

"A-are you trying to tell me you think there are ghosts at Diablo?"

He shrugged, but wouldn't meet her eyes, turning instead to fuss with the equipment scattered at their feet. "I don't know nothing about no ghosts. All's I can say is there's something out there. That's for damned sure."

TAYLOR MADE HER WAY up Main, the strange words of the store's owner rattling her more than she would have liked. Jack had never said anything about odd goings-on at the ranch, and she was sure that if he'd known, he would have told her. It seemed curious that Cole hadn't mentioned the gossip, either.

Which was exactly what it was, of course. Taylor didn't believe in ghosts or anything like that. She was a practical woman. There were explanations for everything, you just had to look harder for them sometimes. Her slashed tires were a perfect example. The sheriff had told her it was probably kids. A group of local teenagers had been running wild lately, and after she calmed down, she had to agree with him. It made sense.

Just like Cole changing his mind did. He'd obviously used his hip as an excuse, so there was a logical, reasonable explanation for why he'd decided to go with her. She'd been surprised, of course, not expecting her plea to really persuade him, but something she'd said had obviously hit home. And she was glad, for more than just the obvious reasons. Once they were at Diablo, maybe it would be easier to hear the details of how he'd gotten them back and what had really happened. Listening to the particulars was as much of what she needed as anything— now that she was strong enough to actually do it. She would thank him, too, for everything he'd done.

Reaching the bottom of Main Street, she turned right and walked the final few blocks to the log cabin that housed the Realtor's office. It sat on the end of the street, all alone. Jim had said the papers might be ready today. If she was going out to the ranch with Cole, Taylor would just as soon have everything taken care of before she left.

The office was empty when she pushed open the door, but a voice answered the bell that had softly announced her arrival. "Be right there. Hang on…"

Putting her purse down on a nearby desk, Taylor looked over the office. At one time, it must have been beautiful. An elaborate Oriental rug covered the wooden floors and once expensive leather sofas were clustered around an antique butler's tray table. The place held an air of disuse now, though, as if it'd seen better times. She walked to the opposite wall to stare at the photos arranged over the coffee-pot. They were old and showed High Mountain as it had been in the 1800s. The town actually looked a little more lively back then, she thought. As she moved down the row, the black-and-white grainy pictures were gradually replaced by more up-to-date photos until finally she came to one that had clearly been taken very recently. It showed Jim Henderson, the Realtor, and a man she thought at first was Cole. She moved closer and stared hard, finally deciding it wasn't Cole. He was tall and powerfully built like Cole, and in his face there were eerie echoes of Cole's features, the Native American costume he was wearing emphasizing his dark good looks. There was something distinct about his eyes, though, a kind of indifference that was missing in Cole's. Standing beside the man was a stunningly beautiful woman. Long, black hair, classic features, eyes that were tilted exotically.

A noise behind Taylor made her turn. Jim Henderson was drying his hands on a tea towel and smiling. He was a trim, nice-looking older man with a wave of gray hair and a beard to match. "Hey, Taylor. You've found my celebrity wall, eh?"

Taylor nodded and returned his smile. "Who is this?" she asked, pointing to the photo of the man who looked like Cole.

"That's Teo Goodman and his wife, Beryl. He's the local Indian Council representative."

"*Goodman?* He sure looks like—"

"Cole Reynolds?" Jim nodded. "They're brothers. Or half brothers, guess I should say. Shared the same mama. Cole's daddy was a local rancher, but Teo's came from the reservation. Their mom was full-blooded—like Beryl."

"Full-blooded what?"

"Jumano Indian."

As soon as she heard that word—Jumano—Taylor remembered. Jack had told her about Cole's background the night before the accident. Fascinated by American Indian art, Jack had wanted to talk to Cole about his heritage, but the conversation had never taken place, she thought sadly.

"It's quite a story, really. The Jumanos were a tribe that lived here in the 15 to 1600s, but by the 1700s they'd been pretty much absorbed by the Apaches and the Spaniards. Interestin' group—into tattoos big time. They lost their whole culture, though. It was a real shame.'' Henderson nodded toward the photo. ''But Teo's doing a damned good job of bringing it back. He's a real hard worker. Setting up schools for the kids, activity centers for the seniors. Raising money for it all, selling cakes and whatnot.'' He dropped the towel to the desk beside him. ''But you didn't come here for local color, did you? You want your papers, right?''

''Are they ready?''

He shook his head. '''Fraid not. Pauline—she's the secretary over at the title company—had to stay home with her grandbaby today, chicken pox, I think, and she didn't get to 'em before she left on Friday. Can you try me again tomorrow?''

Taylor's impatience flared, but for the second time that morning, she reminded herself of where she was. ''All right, but I'm going out to the ranch early tomorrow. I'll be gone for a day or so.''

''Even better, then. We'll have it all fixed up by the time you get back.'' His smile faded slowly. ''But why on earth are you going out there, honey? Won't bring you anything good, that's for sure.''

''I—I just need to, Mr. Henderson. It's one of the reasons I returned. To…to say goodbye, I guess.''

''Well, I suppose that makes sense.'' He nodded his head slowly, thoughtfully. ''I'll have those papers ready just fine, I promise. Don't you worry. We'll take care of everything.''

He'd used the exact same words when she'd been

in before, but she wasn't going to get upset. It didn't really matter. She'd waited this long, a few more days wouldn't kill her. She nodded, then turned to leave. But with her hand on the doorknob, she stopped and looked at the man behind her. "Jim..." She started, then faltered.

He looked up, a curious expression on his face. "Yeah?"

"I know this may sound dumb but..."

"What?"

"I was down at Pearson's a few minutes ago, and Earl Pearson told me he thought the ranch was haunted. Have you...have you heard anything like that?"

From across the room, the real estate agent stared at her. He took so long to answer, she started getting nervous, then he spoke. "Haunted? Why would he say something like that?"

"Actually, I was hoping you might explain it. He said everyone around here knew about it. Something about strange lights, noises..."

"Well, Earl's a weird character. Who knows where he got that idea? I wouldn't let it bother me if I were you."

"He said no one around here would ever buy Diablo."

"Well, he *is* right about that, even if he's got the reasons wrong. No one around here could afford it. We'll find our buyer in Dallas or Houston. Maybe even out of state. Those people from South Carolina like huntin' Texas deer, and they got plenty of money right now.'' He smiled amicably. ''Don't worry about it, honey. Someone will want Diablo, haunted or not.''

SITTING ON THE FRONT porch and watching the sun go down, Cole let his hand drop over the side of the rocker where it landed on the head of Lester, his black-and-tan hunting dog. Easing his fingers over the animal's slick, silky fur, Cole smoothed back his ears. The dog moaned with pleasure, then flopped closer to his master's chair and exposed his belly, hoping for a better scratch. Cole looked down at him and spoke. ''Forget it, partner. I'm too tired to bend over. This is all you're getting tonight.''

The dog yawned, as if to show his indifference, then he rolled over and started to snore.

''And tomorrow night's gonna be even worse.'' Cole spoke out loud, but he was only repeating the words he'd been thinking all day long. He didn't know what had gotten into him at Pearson's. Without any warning, his mouth had voiced promises he wasn't sure his body could keep. He reached for the beer he'd brought outside with him and took a long, thirsty gulp.

He was crazy, pure and simple crazy. If Taylor Matthews wanted to get herself all upset—or worse—what business did he have trying to stop her?

None. But if she went on her own and got hurt

or worse, he'd have to go get her anyway. Accompanying her just made things easier. Lester groaned in his sleep, and Cole stared down at the dog, his shoulders suddenly slumping. Who was he trying to fool? The real reason he was taking her to Diablo was a much simpler one. He'd never forgive himself if something happened to her, and that possibility definitely existed. He'd done the only thing he could. But he'd pay for it...oh boy, would he pay for it.

Almost on cue, his hip began aching. This time of year it always hurt more. The colder evenings seemed to irritate it, and when it rained, the pain got even worse. They were probably going to have both over the next few days. Rain and cold. A front was coming down from the north. They'd catch the brunt of it, he was sure. He knew by now even the weather wouldn't make a difference to her, though.

He turned his head toward the west. Toward Diablo. Taylor was a determined woman...he only hoped he could keep her a safe one.

WHEN TAYLOR MADE her way to the Blazer early the next morning, it was still dark. And in High Mountain, dark really meant dark. Not a single light shone anywhere on Main, and beyond that, into the desert and the hovering mountains, the lack of illumination was even more intense. She glanced uneasily around the parking lot, remembering the slashed tires and silent phone calls. Nothing else unusual had happened so she assumed the sheriff had taken care of the teenagers. She put her nervousness behind her and got into the Blazer.

Forty-five minutes later, she spotted the cutoff to Cole's place, the drive outlined with luminescent markers. She swung the truck off the highway and angled it between the pale green signs to rattle over the cattle guard. A few minutes later, she pulled up in his yard. A weak light came through his window. A dog rose and began to bark as she shut off the engine.

Cole appeared at the doorway, his silhouette tall and forbidding in the darkness. "Hush now. You hush, dog." He wore jeans and a down vest, and in the diamond-hard silence, his voice was low as he spoke to the animal, little puffs of breath coming with it to catch the light. She stared at him for a moment. He wasn't the kind of man she'd ever been interested in—he was too rough, too masculine—but something about him intrigued her. As she watched him bend down and touch the dog's head, she wondered about her assessment. Maybe, in fact, what was intriguing to her were his contradictions. He *was* masculine, *was* rough, but underneath that exterior, she sensed a softer side.

He walked to the edge of the porch, and she got out of her truck, leaving her questions behind.

"I'm not quite ready," he called out. "Come on in and have a cup of coffee."

She nodded, then grabbed the bag she'd packed

with a change of clothing from off the front seat. Crunching across the graveled drive, she smiled at the dog who came down the steps to greet her. "And what's your name?" she asked, holding out her hand.

"That's Lester. He'll be going with us, if you don't mind."

"I love dogs. I'll enjoy his company." She reached the bottom step and looked up at Cole, the hound, sensing a friend, wriggling beside her with ecstasy. "I can't have one of my own—Richard's allergic."

Cole nodded, then turned and went back inside without further comment. Taylor followed.

"Coffee's in there," he said, tilting his head to what she assumed was the kitchen. "I'll just get the rest of my gear and we'll be on our way."

She nodded, then looked around, curious to see how Cole lived. The first time she'd been in his home she'd been too upset to notice her surroundings. Now she saw the cabin for what it was. Peaceful. Calm. Secluded. He'd filled the tiny place with what Taylor thought of as "man" furniture. A deep couch, a plaid recliner, tables with sturdy legs and lamps that were made to read by. She went into the kitchen and saw more of the same, Lester tagging at her heels.

A small pine table rested beside two broad windows, and on the stove, a blue enameled pitcher gave off aromatic steam. It was coffee—boiled on the range and probably stronger than nails. She took one of the ceramic mugs hanging on hooks under the nearest oak cabinet and poured herself a cup. Instantly memories flooded her. Her dad had made coffee this way—they'd been too poor to have a fancy coffeemaker and even if they had been able to afford it, Sid Smithers wouldn't have wanted one. He'd believed in doing things the old-fashioned way. Closing her eyes, Taylor brought the cup to her nose and breathed deeply. As she took a sip, she heard her father's voice and felt the cold bluster of the Montana winds—and the sense of regret it always brought with it.

When she opened her eyes, Cole was standing in the doorway, his dark gaze trained on her. The dog stood in between them, his ears perked, his head swinging back and forth to look at one then the other. The moment could have been an awkward one—she had no idea how long he'd been standing there, watching her—but it wasn't. Just the opposite, in fact. Something in Cole's quiet presence soothed the nerves she'd hadn't really realized were so jangled until now. As soon as she understood the feeling, however, she felt it flee. She spoke to break the silence.

"I love your coffee." She lifted the cup. "I haven't had it brewed this way in a hundred years."

"I'm on the trail so much, I get used to fixing it that way." Walking into the kitchen, he ran his hands through his thick, black hair, pushing it back off his face. Pausing beside her, he reached for one of the mugs. "Can't drink it any other way now."

He was standing so close that above the aroma of coffee, she could smell his soap. She looked up, her eyes studying his face. He'd nicked himself shaving, a small red line marking the edge of his jaw. Unexpectedly, she had a mental image of him standing in front of a steamy mirror, his shirt off, his black eyes focusing on his own reflection, a steady hand scraping a razor across his face. Something twisted deep inside Taylor, and it took her a moment to recognize the feeling as attraction. Shocked, she cut it off instantly and chastised herself. She was practically engaged, for God's sake. What did she think she was doing?

She turned, putting down her mug unexpectedly hard, hot coffee splashing onto the counter. Grabbing a nearby kitchen towel, she wiped at the spot furiously. "Are you just about ready?" she asked, her eyes never leaving the counter.

He took a minute to answer. "I'm ready," he said finally. Taking the towel from her fingers, he draped it over the kitchen sink then turned and went out of the kitchen. Lester glanced at Taylor apologetically, then jogged behind Cole, his toenails clicking on the polished wood floor. She stood in the silence for a moment more, then she followed the man and the dog.

THE SUN WAS HOVERING just above the horizon as Cole pulled the truck up to the metal gate marking the ranch's northwest boundary. A low line of blue clouds hung above them, their ominous darkness coloring the vista with threatening shadows. In the background, near the mountains, flashes of lightning darted across the sky. The cold front was definitely heading their way. Cole turned to the woman sitting beside him. With each passing mile, her tension had risen a notch. He'd sensed it in the closeness of the truck's cab, just as he'd been aware of her perfume.

"This is it," he said, nodding toward the dusty terrain beyond where they sat. "Look familiar?"

She leaned forward, her hands on the dashboard, the pink, buffed ovals of her nails glimmering in the dusty dawn light. "Not really. I don't remember much about that morning." She pointed to the metal sign above the cattle guard. "Was that there?"

"The sign? Yeah. It's always been known as Rancho del Diablo. I guess the previous owners must have put that up."

Black metal stretched in an arch fifteen feet above the cattle guard. The letters that spelled out Rancho del Diablo were weathered, polished into a shiny finish by the constantly blowing winds. Miniature pitchforks decorated each end of the sign.

She suddenly looked uncertain. On the way over, she'd repeated Pearson's gossip. It was clear she didn't actually believe it, but the story had her spooked. Cole could have used her nervousness to try and change her mind, but he knew it would have been a pointless exercise. He'd just done his best to settle her down. If the truth was known, he had plenty of questions himself about Rancho Diablo. He didn't believe in ghosts, but something *was* wrong with the ranch. His own place bordered Diablo, and he'd never gotten accustomed to seeing lights moving across the landscape at night or to hearing the occasional bark of a rifle. All he'd finally done was ignore it.

"It's not too late to forget about this," he said softly. "We can drive right back to High Mountain. It's your call. We can stop and—"

She stared straight ahead and shook her head. "No." Her voice was faint. "I want to go on."

He nodded without a word.

The truck bounced over the cattle guard, the horse trailer behind it echoing the sound a moment later. Taylor gripped the seat and leaned forward. Every muscle in her body was tense and knotted—he could tell by the way she held herself.

"How far does this road go?"

"All the way across the ranch but we'll only take it to the top of that plateau." He pointed to the ridge in front of them. It was the beginning elevation to the mountains behind. "We'll ride in from there."

"How far to the canyon after that?"

"An hour or two, depending on the weather."

She seemed to notice the growing clouds for the first time. "Do you think it's going to get bad?"

"Could happen." He glanced northward. The billowing blackness was beginning to roil. "I brought slickers. We'll be okay."

"It was really hot that day, wasn't it?" Her voice was detached, remote.

He shot her a look. Her profile was soft, almost blurred. Lavender shadows darkened the skin beneath her eyes, and under her cheekbones, there were hollows he hadn't seen two years ago. He wondered suddenly what Jack Matthews would have to say about her returning.

She turned when he didn't answer. "It was hot, wasn't it?" This time her voice was sharper.

"Yes," he answered quietly. "It was hot and that was bad. It made you lose more blood than you would have if it'd been this cold."

She fixed her gaze back out the window, and for the next half hour only silence filled the truck. Which was just fine with Cole. The road hadn't gotten any better over the years, and at times, it took all his concentration to follow it, the trailer bouncing along behind them, Lester adding an occasionally sharp bark to the rattle and jingle of their very slow progress. Cole stole a look at Taylor now and then, but she seemed to be in another world altogether.

Or in another time.

After what seemed like a long stretch, he finally turned the truck's wheel sharply, then eased it up the last incline. Taylor's fingers were now digging into the upholstery, her knuckles white with strain. Brackets had formed on either side of her mouth, and Cole found himself wanting to reach over and smooth them out with his thumb. They were just too painful to see. Instead, he directed the truck into a stand of mesquite and cut off the engine.

Instant and total silence enveloped them, quiet so thick Cole was sure he could hear Taylor's heartbeat if he listened closely. Turning toward her, he spoke, breaking the empty stillness.

"This is the end of the road. We'll have to saddle up and ride from here."

CHAPTER FIVE

COLE GOT OUT of the truck and circled back to the horse trailer. Taylor sat perfectly still.

Ever since they'd crossed the cattle guard and come onto the property, she'd begun to second-guess her decision. What did she think she was going to find out here on this vast, unforgiving land? Peace and quiet? A calm acceptance? Tranquility?

Her heart began to pound and a wave of dizziness hit her. From behind the truck, the dog's excited whines and the soft whinny of one of the horses broke the silence. The sounds seemed to be coming from a long way away, and unexpectedly the warm enclosure of the truck turned stuffy. Pushing up the sleeves of her sweater, she rolled down the window, propped her arm on the cold metal and sucked in the sharp, clean air. Without any warning, Cole appeared beside the door. He peered in the window at her.

"You okay?"

Her voice was terse. "I'm fine."

"You don't look fine."

She turned and met his gaze. His eyes were as black as ever, but there was something else in his stare...something that looked suspiciously like concern. She swallowed hard. "I—I'm a little shaky, I guess."

He'd put on leather gloves to saddle the horses, worn gloves with the fingertips cut out. Lifting one hand, he placed it on her arm, the rawhide soft as cashmere, the exposed ends of his finger unexpectedly warm against her skin. "What did you expect?" His voice was not unkind. "This place holds a hell of a lot of memories. You're stirring up some powerful stuff."

She nodded and bit her lip. "It's what I wanted, but I wasn't prepared, I guess."

He stared at her a moment longer as if he were trying to decide what to do. Finally he reached inside and opened the door. "Come on out, then," he said with a sigh. "We might as well get started before that front gets any closer."

She slipped out of the truck, her boots sinking into the soft, red dirt. A movement near the rear of the pickup caught her eye, and she saw that he'd already unloaded the horses. A black quarter horse stared curiously back at her, twin plumes of steam coming out his nostrils. He snorted softly then nosed the smaller, gray Appaloosa beside him as if to point out Taylor's appearance.

"Kinda late to ask, but you *do* ride, don't you?"

Nodding, Taylor looked up at the man beside her. "It's been a while, but yes, I can ride. I grew up on a ranch in Montana."

He raised his dark eyebrows in surprise. "I thought you said you were a city person."

"I am. I left Montana when I was eighteen and never looked back. I imagine I can still ride a horse, though."

He looked down at her as though he wanted to know more, but he wouldn't ask. Cole Reynolds was the kind of man who respected privacy. Taylor liked that in a person. Especially if it was *her* privacy at issue. An image of Richard flashed into her mind. He'd wanted to know everything about her. How she and Jack had met, where she'd lived before they'd married, where she'd gone to school. Everything.

Without dwelling on the thought, she brushed past Cole and went to the small, gray mare. Taylor allowed the animal to smell her palm, the velvety nose of the horse dry and warm against her skin. The touch brought back memories of her childhood, of rocky crags, and deep snow, and endless sky. Other memories came, too, some of them not as nice.

Cole appeared behind her, patting the smaller horse. "This is Honey, and this fellow over here—" he walked to the black horse and scratched him behind his ears "—is Diego." At Cole's touch, the horse neighed his pleasure then lowered his massive head and nudged Cole's shoulder. "We've been a team for quite a while."

"Why didn't we ride to the canyon that day? Why did we walk?"

Cole pulled a saddle out of one of the compartments built into the side of the trailer, then reached in for the harness and tack. "Your husband didn't want to ride. He told me he wanted to walk the land, said he'd get a better feel for it." Slipping the reins over Honey's head, he stared at Taylor. "Maybe I should have insisted on horses."

"Why?"

He shrugged. "I don't know. Things might have gone differently. It would have been a damned sight easier to get you out of there, that's for sure."

Taylor's chest tightened, seemed to close around her heart a bit. She told herself this was exactly why she'd come back—to hear things like this—but that didn't make it any easier. She took a deep breath. "How *did* we get from the canyon back to the truck? I...I don't remember."

Draping a second bridle over his arm, Cole reached in and pulled another saddle and blanket from the trailer. He walked over to the black horse and dropped the gear by the animal's hooves. Finally he looked up and met Taylor's eyes, speaking reluctantly. "I carried you out."

For a moment, all Taylor could do was stare at Cole. Then she found her voice. "You carried me out? How in the world did you manage that? You'd been shot—we were miles out. How—"

"I slung you over my shoulder and walked." His voice was matter-of-fact. "When that didn't work any longer, I made a travois."

She gripped the edge of the trailer, the cold metal

biting into the palm of her hand. *When that didn't work any longer...* He didn't have to elaborate—she knew exactly what he meant. When he'd lost too much blood himself to carry her. When he'd turned weak and filled with pain, too. The image left her feeling ill.

"How did you manage?" Her voice was a whisper.

He stopped what he was doing and looked up at her. The horse standing between them neighed softly, feeling the tension. "I did it like I do everything," he said. "I took it one step at a time."

"But you were wounded."

He turned back to the horse, waited a moment, then pulled the cinch. When he stood up and looked at her again, his expression was closed. "Don't make it into more than it was, okay, Taylor? I did what I had to do to get us both out of there—what anyone would have done. There weren't any other options."

He was obviously uncomfortable with the conversation, and Taylor didn't know if it was because he was being modest or if he hadn't come to terms with what had happened, either. She nodded slowly. "I don't know if I agree with you—that it was what anyone would have done—but I do know one thing." She paused, waiting until his eyes met hers. "I appreciate it. You saved my life. I—I don't think I ever really thanked you as I should have, and it's long overdue."

For a heartbeat, all they did was stare at each other, the wind at their backs, the quiet stillness of the land surrounding them with an intimate and silent vista of isolation. It felt as though they were the last two people on earth.

"You're welcome," he said finally, his deep, rumbling voice echoing through the emptiness.

A FEW MINUTES LATER, Cole watched as Taylor grasped the horn of the saddle and swung herself up to Honey's back. She seemed a lot calmer, a lot more at ease, and he began to wonder if part of her nervousness had simply been an uneasiness at being around him. They were like two strangers who'd been trapped in an elevator during a storm and then suddenly freed. People didn't always know how to handle the bonding that came with sharing a trauma, especially when the trauma was over. He'd seen the same thing happen between men in his unit during his time in the military.

Eventually, though, she'd have more questions and he didn't want to give her the answers. Remembering the details did nothing for him. He didn't want to have to explain how he'd ripped off his shirt and bandaged both their wounds. How he'd waited out the endless hours for the cover of darkness. How he'd then taken painful step after painful step and gotten them back to the truck, struggling to stay conscious himself, sick with concern that she'd die before he could get them out or that whoever had been shooting at them would come back and finish the job.

It didn't take much effort to recall the agony of driving them to the hospital, veering from one side of the road to the other, praying—for the first time since he was a kid—for help.

He didn't want to remember any of it.

Cole put his boot in the stirrup and swung himself to Diego's back. His memories of their time together two years ago were mostly hellish, but the parts that weren't…well, he didn't want to remember them, either, but they haunted him even more.

When he closed his eyes at night, he could still see the creamy white shoulders, the rapid rise and fall of her breasts, the painful look of tragedy those beautiful green eyes had held. He'd felt like the worst kind of creep when the memories had first come to him. At the time, when he'd bandaged her with the remnants of his shirt, he'd been too concerned about keeping her alive to notice anything, but later, much later, the details had come back to him. The lace of her bra, the blue veins beneath her skin, the perfection of her body. What kind of man wouldn't have noticed? Only a dead one, he'd decided later.

Now, watching Taylor rein Honey into a turn, her jeans stretching tight against the curve of her buttocks, her arms lifting gracefully, he realized once again what a beautiful woman she really was.

And just how different their two worlds were.

He touched Diego's flank with his heel and set the horse into an unexpected trot, Lester beside him. Within minutes, Taylor had Honey cantering beside them. They spoke little over the next hour or so. Cole concentrated hard on making sure he was taking them the right way and not having thoughts he shouldn't. Taylor was clearly concentrating on keeping Honey in line, the horse a gentle one but a handful for someone who was out of practice riding. From time to time, Cole glanced over at Taylor. She'd disappeared into another world, just as she had done earlier in the truck.

By midafternoon, a steady, cold rain had begun to fall. Cole dug out slickers and tossed one to Taylor. She draped it over herself, the bright yellow coat covering her completely. An hour later, his hip screaming, Cole reined Diego to a halt and spoke over his shoulder. "There's a cave about three-quarters of a mile up ahead. I think we need a break."

His voice obviously bringing her out of a daze, Taylor blinked her eyes then nodded as he indicated the direction. Gritting his teeth and squeezing Diego into a canter, Cole headed up the rocky slope, Honey's shoes clacking on the hard ground close behind. They rode directly into the cave.

Taylor groaned as she slid off the horse. "I'm not in as good a shape as I thought I was. My legs are killing me."

Dismounting, Cole nodded, his hand going to his

hip and massaging it under his slicker. He tilted his head toward the north. "With this storm rolling in, we might want to rethink our plans. We could sleep here tonight and have some cover. Get to the canyon early in the morning."

She followed his stare with her own. "Do you think it's going to snow?"

"Could happen." He faced the cave's opening and watched the billowing black clouds. The temperature had probably dropped ten degrees from when they'd left. "We usually don't get it this bad this soon." He turned and looked at her. In the eerie black light of the coming storm, her eyes were even greener than before. "Are you in a big hurry or would you like to take it easy?"

She kept her expression blank. "I've waited two years. Another eight hours won't make any difference."

THE STORM CAME IN just about the time Cole got the fire going. At the mouth of the cave, Taylor watched as the now dark sky filled with lightning. It wasn't the kind of lightning she was familiar with. These were angry slashes that ripped into the black night, then stayed longer to blaze across the landscape. One flash would hardly finish before the next began, the accompanying thunder so loud she could feel its echo in her body. The ferocity disturbed her. She retreated back into the cave and away from the opening.

On the other side of the small enclosure, Cole watched her movement from beneath hooded eyes, the dog at his feet. He'd said little during their ride, and she was grateful for his silence. He'd probably sensed that making small talk was the last thing she'd come to Diablo to do, but somehow now— with the storm outside—she needed conversation, wanted human contact.

She sat down just outside the bright ring of light the fire gave off. Behind them, in the darker recesses of the cave, the horses were restive, the wild weather making them as nervous as Taylor. Shuffling, they made low, munching sounds as they ate. She turned back to Cole and spoke quietly. "You said you've had Diego a long time. Where did you get him?"

Cole took a sip from the coffee cup he held before answering. They'd already had their dinner, thick ham sandwiches Cole had made before they'd left and an unexpected touch—fresh strawberries. "He was a gift," he said slowly. "From my half-brother."

"Teo?"

He jerked his head up in surprise. "You've met Teo?"

She shook her head. "No, but I saw a picture of him in Jim Henderson's office. At first I thought it was you, then I asked and Jim told me who he was. There's a very strong family resemblance, isn't there?"

"We look alike…but that's about it." His voice

held traces of something she couldn't quite define, and his expression shifted slightly.

"You don't get along?"

"Why do you ask?"

"Just the way you said that, I guess."

He answered carefully, as if he were picking the perfect words. "We don't see eye-to-eye on some things."

"Well, you know what they say...you can choose your friends, but you can't choose your family." She waited for a reaction, but the man on the other side of the fire said nothing. "His wife is certainly beautiful. She's Jumano, too, right? I think Jim said her name was—"

This time when he spoke, his voice was flat. "Beryl. And yes, she's Jumano. Full-blooded. Both her parents are Jumano."

Taylor found herself staring at him with fascination. The harsh planes of his face had aligned themselves into a taut blankness that was totally without expression, and he held himself with such rigidity he looked as if he'd explode should she touch him. Obviously this woman meant something to him— the strenuous effort that he was making to cover up his reaction gave it away as clearly as if he'd spoken. Taylor didn't know what to do.

As it turned out, she didn't have to decide. Cole spoke again. "Teo's very big with the local Indian Council, and without Beryl, that would never have happened."

"Why not?"

"Her father was in charge of the council before Teo took over. Without his father-in-law's advocacy Teo wouldn't have gotten where he is now."

"But, I'm sure he's very capable, too. You have to have a certain type of devotion to do that sort of thing."

A hint of cynicism crossed his face at her words. "Oh, he's devoted, all right. You could definitely say he's devoted."

Taylor wasn't sure how to respond to the bitter tone in his voice so she did the only thing she could. She ignored it and changed the subject. "His wife is certainly beautiful. Such long black hair and handsome features, very striking. Tell me more about the Jumanos—"

Just at that moment, an extra-loud clap of thunder rumbled into the cave. Lester raised his head and looked toward the opening and the horses whinnied nervously, but the sound hadn't even faded when Cole rose suddenly, startling Taylor with the quickness of his movement. "We're going to have a long day tomorrow. I think I'll turn in."

Blinking at his unexpected pronouncement, Taylor looked up at him in surprise, but his expression gave away nothing. "Oh…well… Maybe I should, too."

"I put your bedroll over there." He indicated the far wall, then pointed toward the mouth of the cave. "I'll be up here." His dark eyes were impossible to read in the dim light of the campfire, but his shoulders were straight across, more tight than ever and fixed in one position.

She started to say something—anything to fill the moment—but he spoke before she could, cutting off any further conversation.

"Sleep well," he said. "We'll start out early in the morning."

HE WOKE INSTANTLY, his body on full alert even before his mind had a chance to engage. On automatic pilot, he turned slightly and saw that Taylor was safe, tucked into her bedroll and still asleep. He reached for the rifle he'd laid beside his own bedroll, then he sat perfectly still and waited.

Something had roused him. A noise, he was sure. Whatever it was, Lester had heard it too. At Cole's feet, the dog had raised his head, his ears standing straight up as he stared out into the night, his body as tense as Cole's.

Cole waited for the sound to repeat itself, but heard nothing. In the thick black silence of the night he made no movements at all. He'd trained himself well—he could have gone on for hours this way.

After a few minutes more, though, with nothing but silence reigning, he relaxed slightly, turning slowly to glance again at Taylor. She had zipped up the sleeping bag to her chest and was sleeping deeply, one hand thrown out toward the dying fire, the other curled under her cheek. Light from the still glowing embers highlighted the golden strands of her hair, and even though he knew he was making a mistake, he allowed himself to stare his fill at her.

Without warning, her earlier words came back to haunt him.

His wife is certainly beautiful... Such long black hair and handsome features, very striking. Tell me more about the Jumanos...

Tell her more? Oh, Cole could have told her more, all right. He could have explained how he'd always been the outcast in his family, with his paler skin, his acceptance in town, his Anglo friends. He could have told her how his mother had always only patted him on the back, but had hugged and held Teo. And if Taylor had really wanted the full story, Cole could have told her just how dearly he had paid for his father's blood that was now running in his veins. But what was the point? All that was history. None of it mattered now. He pushed the image of Beryl's face from his mind.

In her sleep, Taylor murmured, pulling his thoughts and his eyes toward her. The sounds were full of distress as if she were having a bad dream, and as he watched, she turned once, her hand going to her shoulder as if to protect it from a blow. He was trying to decide if he should wake her when it suddenly didn't matter. A gun boomed in the distance, rapid-fire and deadly. Lester jerked his head up, then froze, the ridge of his spine going hairy and stiff. It was quiet for just a second, then the weapon sounded again. Cole jumped to his feet and Taylor sat up, confused and disoriented.

"Cole? Wh-what was that?" Her eyes were huge with fright as she blinked from the rude awakening. "It sounded like gunfire...."

"It was," he said grimly. "Wait here. I'm going to check." He looked at the dog. "You stay."

Kicking dirt on the last of the embers, he walked quickly to the opening of the cave, his rifle at his side.

The night was dark and cold, much colder than it had been when they'd come into the cave. Tucked into the small cavern with the fire going, he hadn't realized how low the temperature had actually dropped. The cold made the silence even sharper, too. The wind was slight, but he could hear it whistling through a nearby stand of mesquite, the branches clicking together, the bark rubbing against itself. With his back to the cave's side wall, Cole stood on the cusp of the opening, his breath coming out in quick, white clouds, his eyes scanning the horizon.

He saw nothing.

He waited, just as he'd waited before, but a movement behind him broke his concentration. His heart thumping despite himself, he jerked his head around and found Taylor at his side, Lester hovering nearby.

"What is it?" she whispered urgently. "Do you see anything?"

"I thought I told you to stay there."

She frowned at him. "This isn't some kind of bad cowboy movie. I want to know what's going on."

"I'll tell you when I know. Please go back."

"Which direct—"

Before she could finish, the sharp bark of a rifle rang out. Taylor gasped at the sound, and without even thinking, Cole reached behind him and tucked her into the curve of his back, bringing his rifle up at the very same time, all his senses on alert, his eyes straining in the darkness. They were in a good position—no one could see them and there was no light to shine from the cave—but he didn't want to take any chances.

Breathing heavily, he searched the horizon through his nightscope, his fingers steady as he adjusted the lens. At the far right of his range, he caught a movement, in the brush, behind one of the larger cedars. Was it a man or something else? Wild ponies sometimes came this way. Whoever, or whatever, it was a good five hundred yards away, maybe more. Chances were, Cole could see them but they had no idea where he was. He waited for more movement.

"Do you—"

He held his hand up and her words died instantly. It was too late, though.

The figure inside the scope turned toward the cave. Cole couldn't see a face, but he saw enough to tell it was a man, tall and well-built. A second later, he was heading straight for them.

CHAPTER SIX

HE TURNED SO FAST, Taylor had no time to react. In one fluid movement, Cole drew her to him, his rifle hard against her leg, the fingers of his other hand closing tightly over her mouth. Beneath her breasts, his chest was a wall, brick-like and unmoving. The intimacy of the contact was so unexpected—and so powerful—Taylor was instantly stunned, her heart leaping into her throat.

His breath was hot against her ear as he spoke. "Grab your bedroll and your pack and go to the back of the cave. Right now."

"But—"

"Someone's coming and he's got a gun. I don't know who he is, and I don't know what he wants, but I don't want you in the way while I'm figuring it out." He looked into her eyes, the heat of his body pressing into hers. "Please do what I'm asking."

Taylor nodded silently, then turned and did exactly what he'd told her to do, her knees shaking so badly she could hardly walk. By the time she wedged herself behind the horses into a small alcove, her heart was pounding so fast she couldn't think straight—or stop the images flashing into her brain. Dust and pain, cold and darkness, another time when Cole had held her as tightly as he just had, fear rising between them... The sound of the guns had brought it all back. She closed her eyes tightly and forced the images away.

After a moment, she opened her eyes and peered around the edge of the recess where she was hiding. The cave was completely dark—only a slightly lighter section showed her where the opening was— but occasional flashes of lightning lit up the area just outside. Two darker shadows, hugging the wall, gave Cole's and the dog's presence away. She told herself to calm down. There could be a perfectly reasonable explanation for strangers to be on her property, in the middle of the night, shooting off guns.

But she had no idea what it would be.

For a few more seconds, all was quiet. Taylor watched Cole's motionless silhouette and held her breath. Then—just as she took her first deep breath—a flash of brilliance split the dark sky and filled the cave with light.

More than enough light to see the man with a gun who now stood at the opening of the cave.

COLE HAD HIS RIFLE at the man's throat before his brain registered who he was looking at. Even after the realization clicked, it took a moment for Cole to react. He seemed frozen, unable to move, his muscles locking. Finally, he lowered the barrel of the gun, air escaping from his lungs in a rush.

"What the hell—"

"Goddamn it—"

They spoke at the same time, their eyes connecting in the stygian darkness. Cole spoke again, his voice an angry slash. "What in Christ's name are you doing here? You nearly got yourself killed."

They resembled each other enough to be twins. Almost. Cole's skin was two shades lighter and Teo was fifteen pounds heavier. They were the same height, however, and had the same black sheen in their hair, the same dark look in their eyes.

"I might ask you the same thing, baby brother. What are you doing, out here in the middle of nowhere?"

"I'm working." Cole stared at his half brother, then let his gaze go over his shoulder to the dark beyond. "What were you firing at?"

"Beryl saw some wolves hanging around the cattle last week. She asked me to come out and scare them off."

"At night?"

Teo shrugged, a movement that explained nothing.

"Cole?" Taylor's voice came from the deeper darkness inside the cave. "Wh-what's going on?"

Teo swung around in surprise and flipped on a flashlight as Cole answered. "Over here, Taylor."

She appeared out of the shadows, blond hair tousled, eyes enormous. Cole could feel Teo's inquisitive look on his back, but he didn't really care. He'd spent too many years trying to second-guess Teo, trying to please him and get closer to him. Now there was such a gap between them, the insurmountable distance no longer mattered...or so Cole told himself.

"This is Teo, my half brother." Cole turned back to Teo. "This is Taylor Matthews. She owns—"

"Diablo," Teo supplied. Reaching out, he shook Taylor's hand as if they were at a cocktail party instead of standing in a cave in the middle of nowhere. "I'd heard you were in town."

She lifted one eyebrow.

"Word travels fast in High Mountain."

"So it seems," Taylor said slowly. "Did I just hear you telling Cole you were looking for wolves? Is it legal to hunt them?"

"If they're eating your calves..." He shrugged. "Guess it depends."

"And does trespassing...depend?"

His features shifted but the change was so infinitesimal Cole was sure Taylor hadn't seen it. He only noticed because he'd studied his brother for years. "No, I'm afraid it doesn't." Teo held out his hands in a gesture of surrender. "You caught me on that one."

His apology disarmed her, just as he'd planned, and Cole felt a twinge of angry resentment totally unjustified for the situation. He knew instantly where the feeling came from; he'd seen Teo charm their mother too many times—to Cole's own detriment—not to recognize the source. He reminded himself this was a completely different situation as Taylor visibly relaxed, the tension going out of her body. "No harm done, I suppose. After all, I'm here to sell it anyway. It doesn't really matter."

"Well, I promise it won't happen again. Especially since I saw no wolves." Teo smiled, then looked over Taylor's head at Cole, his eyes suddenly unreadable in the dim glow of the flashlight. "I'll see you later, little brother. Stay calm."

He turned and slipped into the darkness, vanishing almost as quickly as he'd appeared. Cole watched him leave, his rifle resting at his side, his eyes narrowing with thoughtfulness as Taylor stood quietly next to him.

Wolves? At Diablo? What in the hell was Teo talking about?

There hadn't been wolves in Rock County for fifty years.

AFTER THAT, it seemed pointless to go back to sleep, even if either of them had been able to. They ate breakfast, then packed up, Cole leading the horses out of the cave, Lester running ahead. Dawn was just breaking as they mounted up and started out. Taylor held her reins loosely and allowed Honey to follow the big black gelding in front of her. When they had moved past the ledge that ran in front of the cave, Taylor spoke, an effort to take her mind off their destination as much as anything. "Were you shocked when you saw your brother?"

"I wasn't expecting him, but I wasn't shocked, either. It's remote out here, but that doesn't mean you can't run into trouble." Cole looked over at her. "Do you see now why I didn't want you to come out here by yourself?"

"But it was your brother—"

His expression seemed to close. "But it could have been anyone."

"Doing what?"

"Who knows? Crossing the river, running dope, hiding out? There are lots of reasons."

"But that's trespassing."

Cole looked at her in amusement. "You think they care about that? My brother obviously doesn't and he's not even a criminal."

"But it is against the law."

"You're right, but in West Texas that doesn't always mean much. People around here have their own code. They believe it's their right to do just about anything they want to, and trust me... trespassing is low on their lists of things to avoid. Unless it's their land, of course."

"And hunting illegally?"

He shrugged. "There's all kinds of wildlife around here. Mule deer, javelina, wild turkeys. People have to eat. They go where the animals are. Use flashlights or whatever they can to spot—"

"Flashlights?" She jerked her eyes to his. "Could that be the reason Earl said what he did? About Diablo being haunted?"

"I don't know. I guess it could have something to do with it."

His voice gave him away—and his expression was even more uneasy. "But you think there's more to it, don't you?"

"I think things are always more complicated than you first believe they are. Diablo has always had a reputation—the locals know that."

"A reputation? What are you talking about?"

He hesitated, then spoke slowly. "The original owners of the ranch—your husband bought it from their estate—were all killed one night. In a fire that wiped out the old ranch house. It happened a long time ago, but people talked it up. Said it was part of the Jumanos' revenge."

"Revenge for what?"

He shrugged, his face a stony mask. "Who knows?"

You do, she thought suddenly. *You know exactly what they meant but you aren't going to tell me, that's for sure.*

She waited, organized her thoughts, then spoke again. "And when Jack bought the ranch and was killed... It only added to the rumors, right?"

"It didn't put them to rest."

She looked out. The rising sun was lighting the horizon, sending a sliver of gold so thin and faint above the rise of the land, she sensed it more than actually saw it. Above the pale, flat line, the stars still shimmered, points of light that dotted the velvet sky. She thought of Jack and how he would have loved to see it and how, unlike her, he would have even enjoyed the rumors of ghosts. Then she resolutely put it all out of her mind. Turning to the tall, taciturn man beside her, she looked into his eyes, as endless as the sky above them, and spoke.

"Diablo isn't a place for rest. It's brought me nothing but pain. Once I sell this ranch, I'll never be back. That isn't a rumor, either. That's fact you can take to the bank."

THEY TRAVELED SLOWLY. The terrain was rockier than it had been the day before, and they were steadily going up to a higher elevation, the air taking on a crystalline sharpness it hadn't held before. Taylor wouldn't have been surprised to see snow.

She glanced over at Cole. He looked completely at home in the saddle, his long legs at ease over the horse's sides, his hands resting comfortably on the pommel. In the cold sun, his hair was so black it held glints of blue, and the shadows on his jaw, where he hadn't shaved, were just as dark. For just an instant, she felt the pressure of his chest against hers as it had been back in the cave, the smell of his fingers as they'd covered her mouth, his voice a throaty whisper against her ear. A moment's guilt accompanied the almost physical memory, and her hands tightened uncomfortably against the reins.

She'd never even looked at another man when she'd been married to Jack. Now she was almost engaged to Richard and having thoughts she shouldn't be having about Cole Reynolds. What in the world was going on?

She turned her thoughts instead to Teo Goodman. Cole had definitely not looked happy to see his brother. A palpable tension existed between the two men, and Taylor couldn't help but wonder about what Jim Henderson had told her. Teo and Cole had shared the same mother but had different fathers. Was that the source of friction between them? She didn't know the answer, but something told her the strain came from a deeper well than even that.

Ahead of her, Cole reached a plateau where he slowed Diego and waited for Honey to catch up. When Taylor reached his side, he spoke. "We're almost there—the canyon starts right over this ridge."

She nodded her thanks, then watched as he nudged Diego into motion and started forward again, Honey following without Taylor doing a thing. Cole spoke as they rode. "Anything look familiar to you?"

Taylor took in her surroundings. At first all she saw were rocks, scrubby trees and endless horizon, then gradually things started to fall into place, to take the same form they had in her memories. She lifted her right hand and pointed to a cluster of boulders. "Over there, isn't that where you stopped to make lunch that day?"

"Yes, it is. You've got a good eye."

She shook her head, dismissing his compliment. "Not really. But that day plays in my mind as though it were a movie sometimes. It'll start at the strangest times, too. When I'm sitting at home reading or just after I've gone to bed. It's almost as if I hear it click on, then I know what's coming. I can close my eyes and see it all. I know I might as well get up and forget about sleeping that night."

Without thinking she reached up and rubbed her shoulder. When his eyes followed her movement, she realized what she was doing and dropped her hand self-consciously.

"Is it hard for you? The memory?"

"Sometimes, yes." She looked over at him, the horses brushing each other's flanks. "And sometimes it's almost comforting." Instantly thinking about what she'd just confessed, Taylor felt herself flush. Richard would have looked at her strangely and asked her when her next appointment with Dr. Kornfeld was scheduled. "Do you think that sounds crazy?"

"It doesn't matter what I think," he answered slowly. "You're the one having the thoughts. Do they sound crazy to you?"

She considered that for a moment, then spoke, almost surprised. "Actually, no, they don't. I think it's a confirmation that I've needed to come here, that I obviously never put it all to rest. I knew it was a problem, but I just couldn't face it until now.''

He nodded, then pulled up his reins, bringing the big black horse beneath him to a gentle halt. Honey stopped as well. ''Well, you've come to the right place.'' He nodded his head to the vista stretching out in front of them, the red, yawning canyon suddenly appearing at their feet. ''This is it. This is where we were when Jack died.''

Taylor grew still, her fingers tightening on the pommel until her knuckles turned white. Beside her, Cole waited.

After a few long moments, she spoke, her voice thicker than usual. ''Sh-show me where we were standing. Exactly, I mean.''

Cole dismounted and took Honey's reins. He reached for Taylor's hand but she saw the gesture of help too late. Already on the ground and standing silently beside the horse, she waited for him as he tied the animals to a nearby cedar.

Cole walked slowly to her side, the sound of his boots loud as they crunched the soil. Putting his hand in the center of her back, he slowly turned her toward the north, to where the canyon lay. Beneath his fingers, under the sweater and jacket she wore, her back was as rigid as a fence post. ''This way,'' he said gently.

She moved, almost in a trance, putting one foot in front of the other, until they reached the very edge of the canyon. They stopped, just at the rim. She faced the gorge without expression, her eyes staring at the endless stretch of land before her. "Leave me alone, please."

After a second's pause, Cole turned and walked away.

Taylor had imagined the moment for so long that she had a hard time realizing she was actually there. She stared at the red rocks and sage bushes with an unblinking eye. Surprisingly, the rush of emotion she'd expected to feel didn't come. With dry eyes and a heavy heart, she stood and waited for it to catch up with her.

Walking closer to the edge of the canyon, she closed her eyes, the wind whistling around her softly, the cold brushing over her skin and biting at her cheeks. She breathed deeply and pulled in the smells of cedar and piñon, of clean air and sunshine. Somewhere in the distance, a bird cried out, the sharp call piercing the quiet. She opened her eyes and stared out at the red rock, twisted trees, land carved by wind and rain and time. For what seemed like a very long time, she simply took it all in, the present and the past mixing inside her.

Then her heart cracked.

And she began to weep.

FROM THE RIDGE overlooking the canyon, with Lester waiting beside him, Cole watched Taylor's still, small figure. She was motionless for quite a while, then she raised one hand and wiped it across her face. The movement seemed to break her trance and she started to walk along the edge, her shoulders hunched against the cold, her hands thrust deep into her pockets. The wind lifted her hair and whipped it into her eyes but she didn't appear to notice, choosing instead to keep her head down and just walk.

He tried to steel his emotions against the pull the sight brought with it. She was just a client, he told himself. A woman he'd known—someone he'd been in a tough situation with, granted—but not anyone who really meant something to him. She wasn't anyone whose troubles he shared.

Then he realized he was arguing with himself too hard.

Taylor Matthews *did* mean something to him, and as much as he wanted to deny it, he couldn't. From the moment he'd seen her, he'd been attracted to her, and besides his first, of course, Taylor was the only woman he'd been unable to get out of his mind when he allowed himself to start thinking of her. She was beautiful, strong, courageous, smart...

And in love with another man.

But even if she hadn't been promised to someone else, it wouldn't have mattered. Taylor Matthews was from a different world—hell, a different planet—than the one Cole Reynolds lived in. She'd never give a guy like him a second look, much less a serious chance.

And if those reasons weren't enough to keep them apart, all he had to think about was how much she hated West Texas. She hadn't said it in so many words, but there were some things a person didn't have to say. The vast open spaces, the hard land, the harsh sky—Cole loved it all...and Taylor hated it. That much was very clear.

He turned away from the canyon and walked toward a nearby rise, forcing himself to focus on the land and not his thoughts.

Nothing had really changed in the two years since he'd last been to Diablo. His eyes went over the horizon, picking out familiar landmarks. He knew the land quite well; before Jack Matthews had purchased it, the former owners had sold hunting leases to it, and Cole had led quite a few men onto the property. They'd never had very good luck bagging anything, and finally their business had died out— the hunting brokers uninterested in bringing executives with deep pockets and handmade Purdy rifles to places where they had no success.

He walked for another half hour, then turned and started back, his thoughts turning to Teo. He'd been up to something last night, but what that was, Cole had no idea. The obvious secrecy made Cole as uncomfortable now as it had when they were kids. He'd always felt as if he were the outsider, with Teo and their mother whispering behind his back. They were constantly sharing secrets and leaving out

Cole. To see Teo do the same now, even though their mother was gone, set Cole's teeth on edge.

He knew one thing. The story about the wolves was just that—a story. More likely, he'd been night hunting, illegal to begin with and out of season to boot. That was the best possibility. Teo liked to think of himself as a stalker, someone who could sense the animals and surprise them with death before they could run. It was all bullshit, of course, but Cole had heard him expound his hunting theories before.

And it was possible he was still out there somewhere. Watching. Waiting. He liked to do that, too. With Lester trotting beside him, Cole topped the nearest ridge and picked up his pace, suddenly anxious to get back. There was no need for Taylor to stay much longer, anyway. At some point, her goodbyes would turn into torture, and that wouldn't help her find any peace. He wanted to get her away before she reached that point.

Crossing a low crest, with the horses finally in view, Cole glanced toward the canyon and stopped. Taylor was back at the edge. Something in her posture seemed different, as if she'd thrown off the tension burdening her. If pressed, he was sure he wouldn't be able to really explain why she appeared that way to him. Maybe it was the set of her shoulders...or maybe it was just his imagination. He hoped not. Feeling suddenly less anxious himself, he took two steps forward then stopped, something shiny and black glinting in the dirt at his feet.

He bent over, his fingers going to the well-packed ground. Whatever it was, the item was embedded, probably had been for years. The blowing winds had finally revealed it, though, and kneeling down to get better leverage, Cole freed it. When he finished, he couldn't believe his eyes.

Lying in the palm of his hand was a small piece of blackened pottery. The sides of the crumbling shard were ragged and dull. It couldn't have measured more than six inches square, but it was big enough. The pattern painted on its side told him everything he needed to know. He'd seen the same distinctive wavy lines on a pot his mother had owned and kept high out of his childish reach.

Jumano pottery.

With one knee resting in the dust, Cole studied the tiny piece of fired clay with amazement. Many times his mother had told him how rare her pieces were, how fragile. With her black eyes huge, she'd explained that the tribe hadn't had the time to make pottery. They'd been forced to move continually, to fight the Comanches for their homes. They hadn't had the luxury of kilns or baking ovens so fired pottery had been an amenity the tribe had little use for.

After their first conversation, he'd wanted to hold her one precious pot, but she'd said no. Taking it down and gripping it carefully in her wide, capable hands, she'd allowed him to touch it, one grubby childhood finger permitted to trace the complex pattern. The next day when he'd come home from school, his mother and Teo had been in the kitchen, their voices low and serious. When he'd understood what they were talking about, Cole had been inexplicably pleased to realize he'd been the first to hear the story…then he'd rounded the corner to see them sitting at the table, the pot cradled in Teo's hands.

Cole closed his fist around the shard, forcing the memories, sharper than he would have liked, into the back of his mind. Were there more pieces here? Could there be a burial mound nearby? He studied the ground carefully but saw no other glints. Who knew what could be beneath the surface?

He stood slowly, a more important question coming into his mind. Did Teo know about this? He was rabid about their heritage, would do anything and everything to protect it. Maybe his appearance last night had something to do with this pottery. Cole thought about it for a moment, then dismissed the idea. They were miles from the cave, and if Teo had known anything about it, he would have already had archaeologists out here, environmentalists, too. No, he didn't know a thing about it.

And if he found out, it'd be disaster. He'd have the place declared off-limits, and Taylor would never be able to sell Diablo—she'd be in court for years, the accident a raw wound that would never be allowed to fully heal.

Cole turned into the chilling wind and slipped the shard into his pocket. He'd have to think about this. Think long and hard.

She looked at him in surprise. "Of course. Why wouldn't I?"

"I thought seeing Diablo might have changed your mind. I know it holds bad memories, but you can't deny its beauty. There's not another ranch around here that big, and the canyon—well, I know you probably hate it, but you have to admit—the view is incredible."

"You sound like Richard."

One eyebrow went up. "He's seen the land?"

Taylor nodded. "A long time ago."

"And he wants you to keep it?"

"Yes—for all the reasons you just mentioned and a few more he's dreamed up. I just can't keep it, though. I don't like it out here…and besides that, as long as I own Diablo, *it* will own me." She sighed. "It's time to move on with my life. I have to."

The clock on the dashboard clicked softly. Outside a dust devil danced between the pickup and the walk running along the rooms of the motel. Taylor spoke again, softly, reluctantly. "I have to admit I was halfway hoping I might change my mind after I went out there—that I'd feel some kind of closure. It didn't work that way, though. Seeing it just reminded me that Jack's never received any justice. The killers just got away. I still feel…as if something's missing."

"You may always feel that way. Sometimes things happen to us and we're never the same afterwards. A chunk of ourselves is gone, and that's all there is to it.''

The words surprised her but watching his face as he spoke, it was clear he was thinking of a situation in his own life, something that had ended wrong, really wrong. She wondered what it was, what part of him was gone. Did it have something to do with his brother?

Would she ever know him well enough to ask him about it?

A few minutes later, he drove away, Lester sitting in the front seat, the horse trailer rumbling behind him. Disappointed and feeling down, Taylor crossed the parking lot and headed for her room, her steps slow and plodding. If only Richard understood, she thought wearily. If only he could see the situation as Cole did. Realizing what she was doing—comparing the two men—disturbed her, but not nearly as much as the discovery of which one was coming out ahead.

Cole, of course.

She forced aside the image of his dangerous eyes and dark intensity, her steps bringing her closer to the door of her motel room, where, she saw now, someone had taped something just above the peephole. It was a sheet of paper, and it was fluttering in the wind and making a whispery sound each time it hit the cheap wood. Reaching the door, she recognized the paper as the want ads from the *Houston Chronicle*. Displayed prominently and outlined in a heavy black border was an ad describing the ranch. Jim Henderson's name and phone number were at the bottom. She reached up to pull off the ad and read it, but as her hand hit the door, it moved slightly, its own creaky hinges adding another sound to the night.

The door to her room was open.

Her heart accelerated, her senses suddenly on alert. Dropping her gear to the concrete floor, she touched the bottom of the door with one boot tip and gave a slow push, every muscle in her body poised to flee.

Her eyes took in the scene and she gasped.

"I DIDN'T SEE NOBODY. I been sittin' here all night and no one's been down there. I woulda seen 'em."

Taylor stared at the motel's manager. She was shaking, her knees actually trembling. She gripped the counter. "If you think I'm making this up, then come down to my room. It's been trashed. Completely trashed! My clothes are all over the place, the mirror is broken, the beds are all torn up!"

"Whaddaya mean?"

"What do you think I mean? Someone's been in there and they've destroyed the room. You need to call the sheriff, and if you won't, then I will."

At the mention of the law, the manager finally seemed to take her seriously. "All right, all right. Lemme see it first."

Taylor led the man back down the sidewalk to the

door of her room, speaking over her shoulder. "I can't believe no one heard this happening."

They reached her door. "The rooms on either side of you are empty but it can't possibly be that—" He pushed it open and his jaw dropped. Taylor looked with him, a sick kind of disbelief welling inside her at the destruction.

Nothing was as it had been before. The bed linens had been torn into rags. The lamps on either side had been flung against the wall—they were cracked and broken and the wall had a big gash in the plaster. The mirror over the dresser, and the one in the bathroom, were shattered. Overlying everything were bits and pieces of what was left of Taylor's clothing. A red silk blouse shredded and draped over the trash can. Her black house slippers sliced to the sole. Even the new down jacket she'd bought just for this trip—but had forgotten in the room—had been ripped and parts of it flushed down the toilet, causing an even bigger mess.

Worst of all was the message smeared on the mirror.

Leave now. While you can.

The man beside her began to sputter. "Ohmygod! What the hell is this? What's going on? The room is destroyed!"

"Is that all you care about?" She pointed to the mirror. "What about—"

"I can't believe this. This is going to cost me a fortune and it's all your fault." He turned toward her, his face alarmingly red, his voice getting even louder. "What are you doing here anyway? If you hadn't come here, this wouldn't have happened!"

Taylor stared at him in astonishment. "Are you trying to blame *me* for this? I wasn't even here, for God's sake! And what do you mean 'if I hadn't been here'?" Her eyes narrowed. "What do you know about all this?"

Up and down the path, doors started opening, men with bare chests and women with frowns staring out to witness the commotion and listen to their conversation.

The clerk's expression shifted instantly and he started to back-pedal. "I—I didn't mean anything. Nothin' at all. Probably a random thing, kids or somethin'." He turned and huffed back toward the office, muttering as he went. "Going to call the sheriff" was all she caught.

Within ten minutes, a white patrol car entered the parking lot, tires throwing up dirt, red-and-blue lights flashing, the siren waking up the rest of the motel for good. The sheriff, a man named J.C. Shipley, stepped out from the left, a deputy from the right. Shipley looked just as he had when Taylor had reported her slashed tires and her ringing phone— as if he had better things to do than administer the law. He frowned as he approached Taylor.

"You found some more trouble, Mrs. Matthews?"

She gritted her teeth at his choice of words, but hid her feelings. It wouldn't help to antagonize the man. "Someone destroyed my room while I was at my ranch. And they left me a message."

Behind them, the deputy had pushed open the door with the end of a ballpoint pen. He whistled when he surveyed the damage, then turning back to Shipley, he shook his head and raised one eyebrow. Shipley looked over Taylor's shoulder and glanced inside. His expression registered nothing beyond mild interest when he saw the mirror, then boredom as he looked back at her. "Tell Joe here your story, Mrs. Matthews. We'll get on it right away." Without another word, he started walking back to his car.

Taylor stood still for just a moment, then hurried after him, her anger and frustration rising up to mix with her exhaustion. "Wait a minute," she said, catching up to him. "You can't just look at that mess, then walk off. I want to know what you plan on doing about this."

He turned and met her gaze. His eyes, small and piggish, looked strange in the motel's neon lights, which were flashing and hissing above them. "I'm leaving it in the capable hands of my deputy, Mrs. Matthews. He handles this kind of thing for me all the time."

"This happens often?"

A look of impatience crossed his features. "No.

All I'm trying to tell you is that he can handle it. You don't need me.''

"Well, don't tell me you think the 'kids' who sliced my tires did this, too? It's obvious—''

He held up one hand and stopped her. "I have no idea who did this, but *like I said,* we'll work on it.'' He put his hands on his hips and glared at her. "Now if you'll excuse me, I need to get back to my office. Joe will take care of you.''

TAYLOR THOUGHT BRIEFLY of calling Cole and telling him what had happened but by the time the deputy finished taking her report and she managed to get into another room, picking up the phone seemed like too much effort. She stuck a chair under the doorknob of the new room. Then, unbelievably, she fell into a deep, dreamless sleep and didn't wake up until late the following morning.

The first thing she did was call Jim Henderson to ask if he'd put the ad on her hotel door.

"Yes, I did, but the door was locked and everything looked fine at the time,'' he said after she'd explained. "I can't believe this. Are you okay, honey? They didn't hurt you or anything, did they?''

"I wasn't even there. I'd gone out to the ranch with Cole Reynolds.''

"Does the sheriff have any ideas who might be involved?''

"No, and I don't think he cares, either.'' She was sitting at a desk in her new motel room, tapping her pen against the plastic top. "But I'm not leaving until I've done what I came here to do."

"Do you want me to pull the ad?"

"No way. I'm here to sell Diablo."

"You sound determined."

"I am and anyone who thinks they can stop me is sadly mistaken."

They talked a few more minutes, Taylor asking the salesman about the old ranch house Cole had mentioned. She'd actually forgotten about it until he'd brought it up.

"Oh, yeah. It's still there—what's left of it, that is. The fire pretty much destroyed just about everything but the foundation and a few beams. Why do you ask?"

Cole's comment about the old house had aroused her curiosity. Jack had had visions of a red-tiled roof and margaritas on the patio, but that obviously hadn't come to pass. "I'd just like to see it," she said simply. "Could I get to it easily?"

"Sure." He gave her directions, then they concluded the conversation, setting up an appointment so she could go in and sign the papers.

"Be careful," he said just before hanging up. "There are some crazy people around these days."

She hung up the phone, nodding her head in silent agreement. *Leave now. While you can.* Still somewhat shaken, she realized she hadn't even mentioned the scribbled note on the mirror, probably, she thought now, because she didn't want to think about it herself. Who would even care that she was in High Mountain? It didn't make any sense at all.

Rising to her feet, she slipped on a sweater and headed outside toward the diner. She'd eat lunch and try to put the whole affair out of her mind.

Thirty minutes later, Taylor looked up from her sandwich and magazine to see a man standing beside her table.

"Mrs. Matthews? Taylor Matthews?" He held a small notebook under one arm and wore a curious expression.

She tensed. "Yes?"

"I'm Bob Hale from the *High Mountain News*. Mind if I ask you a few questions?"

Before she could answer, he slid into the booth opposite her. She started to object, then realized the pointlessness of it. Along with his worn jeans and battered denim jacket, he wore an air of dogged determination that looked as if it'd always been a part of him. She spoke reluctantly. "What can I do for you?"

"I was listening to my police scanner last night when I heard about your motel room. The manager seemed pretty shaken up. I had also heard about your sliced tires and crank phone calls. What's going on?"

"Good question." She met his inquisitive gaze. "But I have no idea."

"Well, could you tell me about the motel room, then?"

"I was gone for a couple of days and when I came back, everything was torn up. My clothes ripped, the room destroyed." She purposely didn't mention the note scrawled on the mirror. "That's it."

"Any ideas who did it?"

"I think the sheriff would be the one to answer that question."

An unhappy expression came over the reporter's thin face, lines appearing to cross his forehead. "The sheriff and I don't always communicate too well."

Her voice turned dry. "Join the club."

He gave her a funny look, then chuckled and relaxed to lean against the back of the booth. "He's not a bad guy, really. Just doing his job." He motioned to the waitress who came over with a cup of coffee. He was obviously a regular. Adding a heaping spoon of sugar to his steaming cup, he spoke. "You really have no idea why this was done?"

"Not a clue. You know High Mountain better than I do. Why don't you tell me why someone would do such a thing?"

He shrugged. "Well...I have heard some rumors. That's why I wanted to chase you down."

"Like what?"

He sipped from his coffee, then spoke. "Like maybe some people around here aren't happy about your appearance in High Mountain."

It took a moment for the words to soak in, bringing with them a wave of nervousness. She forced her voice into a calmness she didn't feel. "Why? Who would even care?"

"The local ranchers for one. Gossip is that you're here to sell the land and that means change—something people don't take kindly to here."

Her throat went dry as she thought about the note on the mirror. "But that's ridiculous. Land changes hands all the time—"

"Not parcels the size of Diablo. Only someone with money could buy that place, and people with money want to make more of it. That means development…a bunch of expensive second homes and everything that comes with it."

"Well, if you ask me High Mountain could stand a little economic boost."

"That's what they thought in Aspen. And in Taos. But when Hollywood found those towns, the locals had to move out. Couldn't afford to live there anymore. Some people think we've got scenery just that nice—and they want to keep it that way."

She leaned back against the booth. "How do they know I wouldn't develop it myself?"

"You're not in the business of developing and they know that. Besides, you've owned it for quite a while and haven't done anything. They like it that way."

Taylor shook her head. "I'm sorry, Mr. Hale, but I don't buy it. It just doesn't make sense. Why try and run me off? Why not make me like the place instead so I'd keep it? Trashing my motel room, slicing my tires, phoning my room at all hours of the night—these are not things that make me want to stick around and maintain the status quo.''

He sucked his bottom lip in and stared at her, his forehead wrinkling in a thoughtful appearance. ''Well, you do have a point there. Maybe we're looking at this wrong. Maybe the locals have nothing to do with it.'' He tapped his pencil against his teeth, then looked at her. ''Could be that none of this has anything to do with selling the ranch. Other things have happened to you out here, haven't they? Really bad things…''

His voice trailed off. Taylor sat perfectly still and looked at him, her breath catching in her chest, her only movement her pulse as it roared through her veins. She was suddenly grateful she was sitting down because her legs wouldn't have held her up had she been standing.

Other things have happened to you out here, haven't they? Really bad things…

Oblivious to her emotional upheaval, the reporter continued. ''''Course I could just be blowing smoke. Chances are you're gonna have a hell of a time trying to sell Diablo anyway. Since the place is haunted and everything…''

She pulled herself together, aware he was waiting for her reaction. ''I—I don't believe in that sort of thing.''

''Plenty of folks around here don't either, but

they've seen the proof. Strange lights, weird noises, things that go bump in the night...you know, ghosts.''

She was blunt, her mind still spinning. "That's stupid.''

"Maybe...but something strange is going on out there. Always has. There's been too much gossip about it through the years to just ignore.''

"And who's spreading this gossip?''

He grew suddenly quiet and looked down at the table.

"Mr. Hale?''

For a moment, she didn't think he was going to answer her, but finally he looked up, gathering his notebook and pen and slipping from the booth as he spoke. "I'm a reporter, Mrs. Matthews. If I went around saying who's talking to me, I wouldn't be in business for very long." He put his hands on the table and leaned closer to her, lowering his voice. "I know one thing, though. Those are the kinds of questions that can get a person in trouble around here. I'd be real careful if I was you."

HE COULDN'T GET HER out of his mind.

Cole fought the memory of Taylor standing on the edge of the canyon, all alone and sad, but it refused to leave. After a night of tossing and turning, he knew he'd have to go into town and find something more distracting to occupy his time than what faced him at home—repairing tack and preparing for his next batch of clients.

An hour later, he pulled the truck into an empty parking space in front of the vet's, Lester cowering in the seat beside him, his tail tucked between his legs as if he knew what was about to happen. Cole looked at the dog and spoke. "C'mon, boy. What kind of cow dog are you? Can't you handle a little ole shot?"

The dog whined his answer and tried to sink lower into the seat, but Cole only grabbed his collar and gently pulled him out of the truck. With toenails dragging on the sidewalk, Lester managed to make the situation as difficult as possible. Just as they were about to go inside the office, Cole stepped back to let someone out and Lester took off.

Cole yelled, but the dog had already stopped. When Cole saw who was petting him, he understood completely. He would have stopped, too.

Taylor had her arms around the excited, squirming animal and was lavishing attention on him. She didn't seem to mind the hair he was shedding on her black turtleneck sweater or even the dusty paw prints now decorating the side of her jeans. With her hair pulled back in a ponytail and the sun shining on the golden strands, she looked like some strange and exotic creature who'd been dropped off by mistake in High Mountain.

She glanced up as he approached. Now closer to her, he could see there were fresh shadows under her eyes and a pale cast to her skin that hadn't been there before they'd gone to the ranch. A cloud of tension and anxiety seemed to hang around her, a cloud that was even darker than it had been when she'd first arrived. It made him want to pull her into his arms and tell her everything would be all right.

His gut tightened at the thought.

"Hi there," she said, standing up and deserting Lester. "What's going on?"

"Why don't you tell me?" he answered quietly. "You look exhausted. I thought going out to the ranch was supposed to set your mind at ease."

"It did. But the coming back got me."

"What are you saying?"

"When I returned to my motel room, it'd been destroyed. My clothes had all been ripped, the room had been tossed. I called the sheriff, but…" She shrugged her slim shoulders in an eloquent movement of dismissal.

Cole kept a neutral expression on his face, hiding the concern that was welling inside him. "Were other rooms vandalized, too?"

She shook her head. "Just mine." Her voice was grim. "And it was personal." She told him about the message.

When she finished, Cole reached over and took her arm, then started back down the street. "Let's not talk about this out here," he said, casually looking around to see who'd been near. "High Mountain's awfully small. We'll go into Doc's office and talk there.''

With the dog trailing unhappily behind them, Cole and Taylor walked into the vet's office. Checking in with the woman behind the desk, Cole led Taylor to a quiet corner where they sat down. Lester curled up underneath their plastic chairs and tried to make himself as small as possible.

''Did you tell Shipley about the message?''

Taylor nodded. ''He didn't seem to care. He said Joe would 'take care of me.''' She took a deep breath. ''That's not what really has me going, though, Cole. I—I talked with Bob Hale afterwards and he implied it might be local ranchers who don't want Diablo sold. He said they hated change and would do anything to avoid it. Then…then he said other things had happened to me out here, too. Really bad things. It…it made me start thinking.'' She finished in a sudden rush. ''What if the things that have been happening to me aren't related to the ranch but instead to Jack's death?''

All Cole could do was stare at her. ''What do you mean?''

Her eyes were huge, two circles of emerald green that reached out and pulled him in. ''What if there was someone who didn't want me around… someone who might be afraid I was here to get the sheriff to reopen the case?'' She brushed a stray strand of hair impatiently from her eyes. ''Don't you see what I'm saying? The person who trashed my room and slashed my tires could be the same person who killed Jack.''

Cole was shaking his head before she had even finished speaking. "Shipley knows who killed Jack and he told you so two years ago."

"He told me who he *thought* killed Jack. He investigated just enough to satisfy anyone who'd have superficial questions later. If I hadn't been injured, I would have pursued it, but I didn't. And after I got home, Richard convinced me that I'd only hurt myself more if I looked into it further."

"And he was right."

She crossed her arms and stared at him. Dim light from a nearby window highlighted the dust motes dancing in the air. "Don't you want to know who shot us? Don't you care about that?"

"It's history, Taylor. Past history. Whoever did it is long gone by now. Besides, finding out who pulled that trigger won't take back your pain." He paused and spoke softly. "Or mine."

"I know. Finding out the truth isn't going to change what's already happened, but if I just leave, just walk away right now, I'll never have any peace in my life." She shook her head. "I'm over my grief, but it isn't enough."

He started to argue and she held up her hand and cut his words off. "I know this is hard to understand. I thought selling the ranch would bring all this to a close for me, but I was wrong." She took a deep breath, her eyes locking with his and sending a ripple of unease down his spine. "The sleepless nights, the anxiety, the emptiness that won't go away—they're due to one thing and one thing only. Not grief. Not anger. Not any of those things. It's justice. It always bothered me that Jack's death went unpunished—that no one was ever arrested and tried for it—but I was so caught up in my grief I didn't do anything about it."

She reached out and gripped his arm, her nails pressing into his skin with urgency, her eyes begging him to understand. "Jack gave his life for me— for us—and his killer was never punished. Staying here and finding out who shot us is the least I can do for him. I owe it to him—*we* owe it to him." She stared into Cole's dark eyes. "I have to find out who killed Jack, and I'm not leaving until I do."

CHAPTER EIGHT

COLE LOOKED AS IF he wanted to argue, but knew it was pointless. Taylor watched the emotion cross his face, then leave, but her gaze stayed where it was and she studied him. His square jaw. His straight nose. The small web of lines near his eyes that hadn't been there when she'd met him two years ago.

His voice, low and urgent, broke into her thoughts. "You're making a mistake, Taylor. A big mistake."

"Maybe I am, but you know what?" She looked at him steadily. "I realized something standing out there on that ledge at Diablo the other day. I realized I put my life on hold for the past two years. Part of the reason was grief and part of the reason was the trauma I went through. A big part of it was inertia, though. Seeing where it all happened did bring me some peace, but I've decided I'm simply not going to live that way anymore. I'm going to *do* something."

"That's fine but if you pursue *this,* you may not be living, period. If these same people killed Jack, and that's a mighty big 'if,' what makes you think they won't try to kill you?''

Her voice was matter-of-fact. "It already would have happened if that's what they wanted. I think they just want to try and run me out of town. Even if they wanted to kill me, though, I don't think they'd take that chance now. I've talked to the sheriff. I've reported everything that's happened. They would risk too much by doing more now."

His eyes were two narrow slits of anger and exasperation. "This is dumb. If you were really looking for peace, you wouldn't be doing this. You're just asking for trouble."

Her indignation flared and she stood. Beneath their chairs, Lester looked up hopefully but sensing more tension than before, he put his head down and inched closer to the wall.

"You don't understand. I thought you did, but you don't. Not really," she said, her voice trembling. "But I don't care. I've got questions that need answers and I'm going to look for them. I'm going back to Diablo, to the old ranch house. And I don't need your help doing it, either." She stared at him a second longer, her heart thumping, her pulse pounding in her ears, then she spun around and left.

COLE PAID LITTLE attention as the vet gave Lester his shot and examined him. Thinking only of Taylor and her "mission," he left the office in a fog. He resented being pulled back into the past with her, and he didn't want to think about the danger she was putting herself in, not to mention him. She didn't understand how complicated life was here in West Texas. People weren't always what they seemed—himself included. He didn't want to think about her, period…but it was too late for that. Way too late. Instead of concentrating on his work—he had a full load of mule deer hunters arriving in two days—his brain was filled with visions of blond hair and long legs. He was just getting into his truck when he heard his name.

Stopping, he slammed shut the door to the truck and reluctantly watched as his half brother crossed the street and came toward him. Sticking his hands in the pockets of his coat while he waited, Cole's fingers found the pottery shard he'd picked up at Diablo. The relationship he'd always shared with Teo was as sharp as the edges of the ceramic pot, as complicated as the design it'd once had. He knew he'd never understand it completely—and frankly, he didn't want to.

"Hello, little brother," Teo said. "Good to see you. Wondered what you were doing since I saw you out at Diablo."

Starting off with a lie, Cole thought. As always. Teo knew everything in High Mountain—some things he knew even before they happened.

"I've been busy," Cole said brusquely. "Going out."

"Season's about to start, isn't it? Got some big white hunters coming in?"

"I said going out—I didn't say with hunters."

Teo nodded slowly. "Aha—the widow, eh?" He smiled, the edges of his narrow lips curling upward, the sun shining on the heavy silver and turquoise beads he wore.

Cole wanted to let the remark pass. He didn't need to get into it with Teo today. He had too much on his mind. Too much Taylor. But something inside him wouldn't let it go. As always. "You don't know what you're talking about, Teo."

They held their gazes a moment longer, two sets of black eyes too dark to read. "The widow's a beautiful woman. Maybe you should get to know her better." His voice was amicable, but Cole knew there was no real friendliness underneath the pretense.

"A little late to play matchmaker, isn't it?" There was a layer of frosty anger in Cole's voice. "Or are you finally feeling guilty after all these years?"

Teo smiled slightly and pretended to ignore Cole's words. "Is she still going to sell her ranch or did she change her mind after seeing Diablo again?"

Cole felt disappointment swell inside him. Disappointment that he could never get a rise from his brother. He nodded reluctantly. "Taylor isn't the kind of woman who changes her mind once it's made up. She listed it with Jim Henderson."

"What's she asking?"

"Why? You wanna buy it?"

"Sure." Teo smiled easily. "But simple black-smiths don't make that kind of money, do they?"

"And what would you do with a ranch like Diablo, Teo?"

"Raise my children, hunt, run a few more cattle than I can manage now...the same thing everyone else around here does."

"But you're not a rancher...just like you aren't a 'simple blacksmith.'"

Teo's eyes narrowed. He dropped his voice as he spoke. "You haven't been around me for so long you don't know who I am anymore, if you ever did. You never come by, never visit. Hell, my kids hardly even know you." He stopped speaking then seemed to pull back, to tuck his anger inside him a little deeper. Cole had a fleeting moment of confusion. Was Teo trying to be friendly or was this something else?

Teo spoke again. "Maybe you should come over for dinner one night. You could bring the widow."

A band of emotion—something he'd rather ignore than acknowledge—tightened around Cole's chest. "Taylor's busy with her own plans—and she has plenty of them. Besides, visiting your and Beryl's happy little home isn't something I'm interested in, either. I would think you'd understand that."

Teo shook his head, studied amazement in his expression. "Twelve years later, and you're still mad at me? We share the same blood. How can you carry your anger that long?''

''It's easy.'' Ending the conversation, as he should have done sooner, Cole opened the door to his pickup and slid inside. ''Just ask Beryl.''

EARLY THE NEXT MORNING, her truck bouncing over the cattle guard at the road into Diablo, Taylor headed in the direction she hoped led to the old ranch house. The sky looked threatening, but she had plenty of time and would be back long before the bad weather broke. She had everything she needed right now—a rough map from Jim Henderson and grim determination, even more than she'd had after talking with Cole yesterday.

Thanks to the sheriff.

She'd gone directly to his office yesterday afternoon and demanded a meeting. Bob Hale had said Shipley was okay, but she had serious doubts about that evaluation. She gritted her teeth, her jaw a straight line of disgust and anger as she remembered the conversation.

Shipley had been ensconced behind his desk, a massive piece of dark oak that had been selected, she was sure, to intimidate. Its size had nothing to do with the amount of work done behind its broad expanse.

''Mrs. Matthews. What seems to be the problem *now?*'' he'd asked.

She'd stood in front of the desk, resolve fueling

her. "I'm here to find out more about the investigation you did in my husband's murder. I heard something in town this morning that makes me think there might be a connection between the problems I've encountered here and his death."

He leaned back in his chair, the springs complaining under his muscular girth. His voice held incredulity. "You're linking vandalism and murder? Where'd you get your criminal psych degree, Mrs. Matthews? You didn't get your money's worth."

She bit back an angry retort. "You never arrested anyone, did you? Never brought anyone to trial?"

"Nooo." He dragged the word out until it contained twice as many syllables as it needed. "We never did arrest anyone...because our primary suspect was a Mexican national. We tracked him to the border, then had to let him go. He disappeared into the interior. We had no way of taking it further."

"You couldn't have had the Mexican authorities arrest him?"

"You can't arrest someone you can't find."

"So he just went free...and you left it at that?"

He picked up a massive fountain pen from the top of his desk and squeezed his fingers around it tightly. After a moment, he dropped it and brought his eyes to her face. "I did everything I could with your husband's case, ma'am. You should have no complaints...especially two years after it happened. If you'd had problems with it, you should have said something back then."

"I couldn't. I was in physical—and mental—therapy for quite a while. The whole incident almost destroyed me. I was wounded terribly."

"So was Cole Reynolds...and he's not in here complaining."

"And no one's trashed his house or sliced up his tires, either."

He waited a moment then sighed. "What is it exactly you want me to do?"

"I want your help. I want you to reactivate the case and look at it more closely."

"I'm not going to do that. For one thing, it's not necessary and besides, it's been two years. Too much time has passed."

"But what about the things that are happening to me *now?*"

"From a *professional* point of view, it's ridiculous to think the incidents are related."

Their gazes locked, the tension in the room so thick Taylor thought she could blink and see it. She took a deep breath and put her hands on the desk, leaning across it.

"I accepted your excuses two years ago, but I'm stronger now. If my husband's killer is still out there and trying to run me off, I'm warning you right now there's going to be trouble. I am not leaving until this is finished. Finished for good."

"There are lots of ways of finishing something 'for good.' I would be careful if I were you."

"I'm well aware of that, Sheriff, and that's why

I came here. I thought you might be interested in stopping any future problems, but obviously I was mistaken.'' Her was heart pounding so hard she was sure he could hear it. She spoke softly, above the roar going on inside her, repeating the words she'd said to Cole.

''Justice was never served in this case. My late husband gave his life for me. The least he deserves for that sacrifice is for the truth to come out. And I'm going to see that he gets it, even if you won't.''

Just then, the Blazer hit some particularly deep ruts, and Taylor's mind jerked back to the present. She gripped the wheel harder to keep from completely losing control of the vehicle, the tires dangerously close to the edge of the steep incline. Glancing out the window, she fought the wheel and managed to wrestle the truck closer to the center of the road, her heart in her throat.

The sheriff had thought she was nuts and so apparently did Cole.

She sighed heavily. She'd believed Cole understood, had compared him to Richard, had even wished Richard had the same kind of sympathy for the situation that Cole did. What had she been thinking? Cole didn't understand it any better than anyone else. She was alone in this, all alone.

The Blazer unexpectedly reached the top of the incline and she brought it to a standstill. Looking out at the unforgiving landscape, in the unhurried cold and brilliant blue sunshine, the sudden realization came to her that in the past two years her life had been so confused, so mixed up that she'd been making some bad decisions. It'd started with Jack's death and included accepting Shipley's lame excuses. And it had continued when she'd allowed Richard to give her the ring.

All at once, her life seemed almost incomprehensible. How could she have been so casual about these things? She'd been sick and wounded, and that explained not protesting Shipley's theory, but she had no excuse for the other. Spending the rest of her life with someone was something that deserved a lot of consideration.

She swallowed hard and put the truck into motion once more, easing it over ground that was a little more stable. At the very least, she would have expected to feel guilty about entering into an engagement with Richard. And she hadn't.

But when she thought of Cole…

Those lips. Those eyes. That hard, firm body.

More and more he was in her thoughts and it was getting impossible to keep him out, despite all her efforts. There was just something about him, something intriguing and appealing. He tried so hard not to care—not for her, not for himself, not for anyone, but beneath the rough exterior she'd caught glimpses of the real Cole Reynolds and he was a man who couldn't help but care. She remembered very clearly her thoughts on seeing him for the very first time. That he wasn't her kind of man.

Maybe she'd been wrong.

She gunned the truck over a rough spot, then guided it carefully between two massive pieces of rock. Coming out on the other side, from the cold shade to the warm sunshine, she shook her head. Peace? Who was she trying to kid? Returning to Diablo and High Mountain hadn't brought her peace. All it'd done so far was make things even more difficult.

And she had a feeling the situation was only going to get worse.

THE RUBBLE ROSE UP out of the red dirt as if it'd been planted there by some long-forgotten farmer who'd used wood and brick for seeds. The fallen timbers and tumbled-over bricks had the look of belonging to the land, of being part of it instead of just placed on top. From a distance, Taylor let her eyes take in the burned-out shell. Then her gaze slipped past it, to what lay beyond.

For as far as she could see, the Texas landscape stretched. Miles and miles of empty land beckoned, not another man-made structure in sight. The ground was bloodred under the merciless sky and Taylor shivered unexpectedly as she stared out the windshield. Even though the beauty was stunning, it seemed as though it were a cruel emptiness to her. There would be no help for anyone lost out here, no comfort, no sheltering arms…nothing but a constant solitude that would eventually steal life as well as sanity. Her gaze went back to the house. What kind of person would want to perch a home at this desolate place?

She surveyed the area in front of her, trying to decide which way to go. There was no sign of a road now. The loosely defined ruts she'd been following had disappeared completely. To the west of the house, there was nothing but air. It seemed as if they'd built right up to the very edge of the ridge, dangerously close. To the east, a group of cedar trees stood sentinel between the looming expanse and where she was. She decided to park there, in their sketchy shade.

Taylor pressed down on the accelerator, but instead of advancing, the tires spun crazily in the loosely packed dirt, small rocks pinging against the wheel wells. She gunned the engine, and for one long heartbeat felt nothing. A second later, the tires took hold and the vehicle shot forward, the steering wheel suddenly spinning in her hands.

She gripped the turning wheel and fought for control, barely managing to bring the truck to the left instead of the right. Her pulse hammering, she navigated the tires over rocks and through wild sage and weeds, their limbs screeching at the side of the truck's door. The cedars loomed larger through the windshield as she grew closer. They were full-grown trees, their characteristically twisted trunks looking tortured against the empty backdrop of the mountains beyond.

Heading toward the largest tree, Taylor picked a shady spot just on the right of the rough-barked trunk to park. She moved her foot to the brake and tapped it lightly…but the truck kept going. Going faster, in fact, picking up extra speed as it began to slide down the incline to where the house rested.

Taylor pushed harder, putting all of her weight behind the effort, but the brake pedal went to the floorboard with a sickening looseness, not slowing the vehicle one bit.

She jerked her eyes to the windshield, her throat closing in fear. The trees were close, too damned close. Praying, Taylor pumped the brake again, once, then twice, her hands gripping the steering wheel with suddenly bloodless fingers.

But the truck kept going. Faster. And faster.

Bouncing over a deeper rut, the Blazer bottomed out, the undercarriage of the vehicle scraping over the rocky soil with a deafening screech. Taylor screamed, the wheel now spinning uselessly in her hands, right then left, left then right. Still pumping the brake, she considered trying to jump, but by the time she had the thought, it was too late. Heading straight for the largest tree, the Blazer surged ahead, the rending sound of tearing metal splitting the desolate silence.

CHAPTER NINE

"COLE, JIM HENDERSON here. I understand Mrs. Matthews went out to the ranch with you earlier, and I was wondering if you have any idea where she might be now. We had an appointment at two, and she didn't show up."

Cole gripped the phone. "Did you try the motel?"

"First thing. There wasn't any answer and her Blazer's not there. I had the clerk check." Silence filled the line. "I wouldn't think anything of this except for what happened to her motel room. You know about that, don't you?"

"Yes." And I blew her off, Cole thought, silently cursing. "Did you call Shipley?"

"No. I didn't think that was necessary just yet." Henderson laughed, a forced sound. "Hell, she might be getting her hair done or something, and then I'd look like an old fool worrying about a pretty young blonde. Thought I'd just call around first before I got him involved."

Cole suddenly remembered her determined look when they'd talked earlier. "I think I know where she might be. She said something about going out to the old ranch house at Diablo.''

"Oh, God, that's right. She asked me for a map to the place, but I never even thought about her going out there alone. I assumed you were going with her.''

"No, no. I didn't go with her, dammit. I should have, but I didn't.'' He took a deep breath and reached for his hat, hanging near the phone by the back door. His voice was flat. "I'll go now, though. If I don't call you back in a couple of hours, call Shipley and tell him where I went.''

COLE REACHED THE GATE leading to Diablo in record time. Turning left after going over the cattle guard, he headed the truck east, not bothering with the ruts where the old road lay. He was in a hurry. He was getting there the fastest way he could. On the seat beside him, Lester scrambled for a foothold as they bounced over the rocks and low scrubs, finally giving up and jumping to the floorboard where he wedged himself against the rubber mat and the door.

In twenty minutes, they were topping the ridge. Cole's eyes searched the horizon, an early dusk making the task more difficult than usual. Finally, in the distance, he spotted the house, and goosing the truck, he headed down toward the burned-out ruins. As he got closer, he made out more details. Empty windows, fallen beams, scorched trees...and a black Blazer leaning at an angle so crazy, Cole felt his pulse take a disbelieving leap.

Tires throwing dirt, engine whining, the truck skidded to a halt as he pulled up in front of the house. Without bothering to shut the door, he stumbled through the rocks and scrubby plants. ''Taylor! Taylor! Are you there?'' Lester ran over the terrain behind him, then shot ahead of him, heading straight for the Blazer. The dog clawed furiously at the crushed and dented door, then began to bark and whine, a high keening sound that made the hair stand up on the back of Cole's neck. He ran to the spot where the dog was digging feverishly and pulled him back, straining to look through the window.

The vehicle was empty.

And there was a streak of blood on the seat.

A cold sweat of fear broke out on Cole's forehead and he rocked back on his heels, his heart hammering. Lester gave him a quick, anxious look, then put his nose to the ground and took off running. He began barking noisily a second later. Cole jumped up and turned around to see Taylor greeting the dog from a nearby stand of trees. He ran to her side, a relief so intense coursing over him that he almost felt weak.

Without a word, she looked up at him. An enormous bruise had already started to discolor her forehead, a bump the size of an egg rising up underneath it. Her makeup was smudged and a long red scratch marred one perfect cheek. Nothing felt more natural than when he held out his arms and she moved into them. He swallowed hard and pulled her tight against him, her quivering form slight and more delicate than he had expected it to be. They stayed locked together for several seconds, then Cole reluctantly stepped back to look into her eyes. They were shimmering green pools of fear and shock.

"Are you okay?" he said softly.

Her mouth trembled, but she nodded her head. "I—I'm fine. Now."

She didn't need to say more. He understood. Pulling her to him once again, he patted her back and murmured words of reassurance, realizing how well they fit together, how strangely complete he felt with her in his arms. Finally he broke the embrace again. He had to or the situation would have turned into something else. Something he didn't want and she didn't need.

"What happened? You forget to use the brakes?"

She smiled shakily. "I didn't forget…they just didn't work."

"Were they soft before you started up here?"

"No. They seemed fine when I left. But when I got to the top of that ridge, the truck got stuck and I had to gun it. By the time I got to the bottom, they weren't working. I'm lucky I wasn't heading toward the other side of the house."

They turned together and looked in the opposite direction—to just beyond the ruins, to the edge of the ridge and the dropoff. The two-hundred-foot dropoff.

Cole turned back, as did Taylor, their eyes locking as a sick feeling passed through Cole's gut. His voice became husky. "You shouldn't have come out here alone."

Her eyes darkened with protest. "It wouldn't have mattered. The brakes would have failed one way or the other."

"Is that what you think happened? That they failed?"

"All I know is I topped that ridge and when I started down, I couldn't stop. If someone tampered with them, I wouldn't have made it this far, would I?"

"Not necessarily. If you'd had a leak in the hydraulic line, the fluid would have seeped out gradually. The brakes could have been fine until the line ruptured."

"And do leaks like that just…happen?"

"Sometimes." He paused. "And sometimes they have help."

In the growing darkness, a sudden burst of wind gusted over them, sharp and biting. Cole felt a sting in it—dust or ice, he wasn't sure which. He needed to get her out of it, one way or the other. "We can come back tomorrow and look when it's lighter. Right now, we better get out of here. If the weather gets any worse, we might not be able to leave and I didn't bring supplies." Against his better judgment, but unable to stop himself, he put his arm around her waist and started forward. She pulled him back, her hand against his arm.

"Cole?"

Looking down at the long, slender fingers, an image came into his mind, the image of that same hand lying on top of the sheets in the hospital two years ago. He'd stared at her hand for hours because he couldn't bear looking at her face, she'd had so many bruises and cuts. As he lifted his gaze to the same face now, standing so close he could smell her perfume, he saw the fresh bruise and a twist of hot anger shot through him. Anger at whoever might have done this, anger at Taylor for being so stubborn, and finally anger at himself for caring so much…for caring *too* much.

"Thank you for coming. It was going to be a long walk back." She put her fingers to her head and felt the bump, grimacing. "Really long."

"You wouldn't have made it," he said bluntly. "And if you'd tried, you would have ended up dying."

Her expression tightened, but he stood where he was, his fingers digging into her waist as though he could make her understand. He jerked his head toward the horizon where a group of ominous clouds were bringing darkness with them. "See that? It's a snowstorm coming in. You don't have on enough clothes, you're hurt, and you have no idea where we are right now."

She started to speak but he stopped her with his stare. "What in the hell do I have to do to make you understand? This isn't the city. You can't just call 9-1-1 and get help. Diablo is a harsh place, a dangerous place. It took your husband and if you don't watch out, it's going to take you, too." He stopped and swallowed hard, his voice going husky and soft, his emotions getting the best of him. "I don't want that to happen, Taylor. I saved you once, but I'm not sure I could do it again."

THEY MADE THEIR WAY out of the ranch and back to the main road, but it wasn't easy. Between the wind rocking the truck, the early darkness, and the sleet coming down in fitful bursts, Taylor wondered if they were going to make it. She wasn't sure she wouldn't have been better off trying to hike out. The tension inside the truck was suffocating, Cole's anger simmering between them as if it were a pot about to boil over. Even the dog seemed to notice. He curled up on the floorboard by her feet and kept his head down.

Cole's words kept playing again and again in her head, though. Was he starting to care for her? Was he having feelings for her? The idea scared her and thrilled her at the very same time.

Still, when he took the cutoff to his house instead of going straight into town, she turned to him in surprise. "Aren't you taking me back to the motel?"

"Look outside," he said grimly. "We're lucky

we got here. I'm not pushing it just to get you to town.'' He cut his eyes in her direction, then back to the road. ''With that bump on your head you shouldn't be alone tonight anyway. Do you have a headache? Hurt anywhere else?''

''I'm fine,'' she lied, turning toward the window. In fact, she ached all over and there was a nasty cut down her right leg. It didn't look as though it needed stitches, but it wasn't pretty.

She wasn't about to explain all that to Cole, though. He *might*, emphasis on *might*, care for her, she thought, but he was still angry and wouldn't want to hear about her silly injuries. And part of her actually understood. His life had probably been just fine before she'd shown up. Now every time he turned around, he had to rescue her—something she didn't like any more than he did. It might not look that way, but all her life, she'd been the kind of person who took care of herself without help from others. She'd had to, especially before she'd met Jack.

The headlights sliced through the darkness and lit up Cole's house. A second later, he directed the truck to the front porch and nodded toward the door. ''You go on in. I've got to feed the animals.''

Without saying a word, Taylor nodded and opened the truck door, a blast of cold air filling the cab. The dog jumped out and Taylor followed, closing the door with a slam and running up to the porch. Cole had already pulled away by the time she got the front door opened and she and Lester were inside.

The house was warm, a lamp shining softly by the sofa, a newspaper spread out over the coffee table in front of it. Cole had explained that Jim had called him and that's why he'd gone to search for her. Obviously he'd been reading and taking it easy when he'd gotten the call. In one corner, the television was still on, the sound of canned laughter coming faintly from its direction. She walked over and turned it off, the room falling silent except for the sound of the wind outside and the ping of ice as it hit the windows. She stepped to the nearest one and looked toward the blurry lights of the barn.

She really didn't want to be here. She was scared and tired. She'd come to High Mountain for answers and all she was finding were more questions. Someone might be trying to kill her and she was falling for the wrong guy. Things weren't looking good.

The lights in the barn flickered then went out. A few minutes later she heard the truck pull up outside the house, then Cole's footsteps on the porch. By the time he opened the door, she was facing him, her features arranged in a noncommittal expression she hoped didn't give away the turmoil going on inside her.

"Everything okay?" she asked.

"Just fine." He shook off the dusting of ice and snow coating his shoulders, then removed his hat, hitting it on his leg to do the same. Shrugging out of his coat, he finally turned to her. "Look, I'm sorry. I had no right—"

"You had every right," she said softly. "Don't apologize."

"I shouldn't have gotten angry, though. My father always said it was the measure of a man to say how he felt without getting all riled up."

"That's not always an easy thing to do."

"No, it isn't," he agreed, his West Texas drawl more evident than usual. "But sometimes things have a way of getting out of hand, and it makes it even harder."

Taylor's heart thudded uncomfortably, yet she couldn't look anywhere but at Cole. In the lamplight, his dark hair gleamed and the line of his jaw was shadowed into a plane even sharper than usual. She reminded herself she couldn't feel anything for this man, reminded herself of Richard, but her body didn't want to listen. Instead, her senses recalled the feel of Cole's hands on her shoulders, the length of his body against hers, the way his breath had warmed her cheek in the cave.

As if he had read her mind and it scared him, too, he turned abruptly and went into the kitchen, Lester with him. Thoroughly rattled, Taylor followed a little more slowly. Cole was leaning over the open door of the refrigerator when she got there.

"I'm not much of a cook, but I can throw something together." He spoke without looking at her.

"The bathroom's at the end of the hall. There's first aid stuff. You'd better clean up that cut."

"I will." She paused. "I'd like to soak, too. If I don't, I'll be in bad shape tomorrow. Do you…do you have anything I could put on instead of these clothes?"

"I'll find you something." He looked up finally. "Can't promise it'll have a designer label."

"I don't need that." Turning around before he could say anything else, Taylor made her way through the living room and down the hall. In the bathroom, leaning against the closed door, she took a deep breath and waited for her heart to slow. What was happening? Was she getting in over her head?

She opened her eyes and told herself she really was going crazy now. Not just depressed, not just anxious. Crazy. Downright crazy. Cole had a smoldering kind of appeal no woman could ignore, but she was not supposed to notice it. What about Richard?

Taylor straightened and began to take off her clothes, pushing her thoughts as far as away as she could. While the tub filled with water as hot as she could bear, she turned to the medicine chest and opened it, locating bandages and antiseptic, too. Wincing and trying not to look too close, she cleaned up her cuts, including the one on her leg which wasn't as bad as she'd thought. By the time she finished her bath, she felt halfway human, her emotions and everything else almost under control again. She stepped outside the bathroom, wrapped in a towel. On his bed, there was a light blue robe, embroidered with flowers and delicate green leaves.

Taylor let the towel drop and reached for the robe. The material was incredibly soft, unlike anything she'd ever felt before. It had the texture and weight of cashmere, but actually felt more luxurious. Slipping her arms into the sleeves, she realized at once it was too big, but she wrapped the belt around her twice and rolled up the sleeves. She told herself not to wonder about the woman it belonged to.

The hem of the robe dragging, she walked into the kitchen. Cole looked up from where he stood near the stove, a spoon in his hand stirring something that smelled wonderful. His eyes roamed over her figure, then without a word, he turned around once more. Taylor stood by the door, awkwardly wondering what to do with herself when he spoke. "There's stuff for a salad in the refrigerator. If you don't mind, why don't you throw one together?"

Grateful for the task, she immediately did as he asked, finding a bowl, getting the lettuce and tomato out, working silently, but very much aware of him every second. By the time she'd finished, he was done, too. Fragrant bowls of stew sat on the table, coffee mugs beside them.

They ate in almost total silence.

Finally, Cole looked up. "I think it'd be best if you went back to Houston, Taylor. As soon as possible."

Taylor was shaking her head before he'd even finished speaking. "I can't do that."

"You've had strange calls in the middle of the night, someone slashed your tires, your motel room was trashed…and now this. How can you sit there and say you can't leave?"

"I owe it to Jack. I've explained already."

"Then explain again because I'm still not understanding."

Wind howled around the eaves, and ice battered the roof. In the fireplace, a warm blaze crackled. In another time and place it would have been cozy, seductive even, but not here and now. There was a knot the size of a baseball between Taylor's shoulders and enough tension inside her to keep it there forever. She took a deep breath and let it out slowly, her voice low and uneven.

"I came to Houston when I was just eighteen. I'd grown up in Montana—on a cattle ranch near the eastern border, to be exact. My father was the foreman. He'd worked his way up from being just a hand to running the place. He loved his job and it meant everything to him. And that's why I had to leave."

Cole sipped coffee. Over the rim of his mug, his eyes were steady and dark, although they'd widened when she'd mentioned Montana. "Go on," he said.

"My senior year in high school, I fell in love—with the son of the guy who owned the ranch. It was a cliché, I know…foreman's daughter, owner's son…but it didn't feel as if it were a cliché. Brad and I really loved each other.''

''But?''

''But, Brad's mom didn't think I was good enough for her son. The summer after we graduated, she told me I had to disappear, or she'd see that my dad was fired and both of us thrown off the ranch.'' Taylor looked out the window. In the reflection she saw memories she hadn't let herself see in years.

After a moment, Cole spoke. ''So you left.''

''Yeah.'' She turned back and faced him. ''It broke my dad's heart when I moved away. He didn't understand.''

''You never explained?''

''How could I? If I'd told him the truth, he would have quit. He was a proud man and if he'd known what she'd done, he would have felt compelled to stand up for me. But he was sixty at the time. How's a sixty-year-old cowboy with no other skills going to find a job, especially a job he loved? He had no reason to keep going except for that. My mom had died two years before and I had no brothers or sisters.''

''So you moved to Houston?''

''Yes. And vowed never again to live someplace where I couldn't see any other lights on at night. I wanted the big city, and neighbors, and coffee shops.''

''So you met Jack…''

She nodded. ''I had some friends who'd gone

there to go to school in Houston. I couldn't afford that, of course, so I got a job the first place I came to—a printing shop that did posters, graphic artist stuff, public relations work. A year later, my dad died.'' She made her voice matter-of-fact. ''He'd had lung cancer and no one even knew about it. I was all alone then.''

''And not yet nineteen?''

She nodded. ''When I got what little money he'd saved, I started taking night classes at the University of Houston. Jack was a guest lecturer for my art history class. He was a fascinating speaker and it was obvious he loved the subject. We spoke briefly the following week, then he showed up one day at the print shop and placed an order.'' She smiled, remembering. ''Later he confessed…he'd asked my art professor where I worked. He hadn't really needed five thousand new business cards.''

Cole put his mug down on the table and looked up at her. ''You loved him a lot.''

''He was the only person I had to love. And he gave his life for me.'' She paused. ''After he died, I wanted to die, too.''

''But you didn't.''

''No. And I know now I won't. I loved him, but he's gone and it's time to move on. I've accepted that, said my goodbyes.''

They sat in silence. From beneath the table, Lester rose, stretched, then ambled over to his water bowl, his collar jangling as he walked.

She didn't realize what she was doing until Cole spoke. "And the man who gave you that ring? Do you feel the same way about him?"

Her fingers froze. She'd been playing with the diamond Richard had placed on her finger, moving it back and forth, pulling it off and putting it back on. She lifted her eyes to Cole's...and said nothing.

After a moment he rose. Walking stiffly to the coffeepot on the counter, he filled his cup then returned and did the same with hers. When he sat back down, she still didn't have an answer. The silence continued until Cole spoke softly.

His voice was husky. "I loved a woman that way once."

She waited for more, but there was none.

"Then you understand," she said. "You lose them and you think for a while that you have nothing left."

All Cole did was nod his understanding. They cleaned up the table, and he disappeared down the hallway. A few minutes later, she heard the shower running. Exhausted and suddenly drained, she sat down heavily in the plaid recliner near the fireplace. The next thing she knew, Cole was kneeling beside her, gently touching her shoulder, waking her up.

"C'mon, Taylor. I made up the bed for you."

His hand was warm and heavy where it lay against the robe, his fingers curling into the softness of it, touching her shoulder beneath. He lifted his other hand and brushed his fingers over the bruise at her temple. She breathed deeply, the clean smells of soap and shampoo mixing with the smoky aroma from the fire and the lingering scent of coffee. An awareness started low in her stomach and worked its way up her body, pulling the energy from her and leaving in its place a lethargic paralysis that kept her from moving.

And then he was leaning toward her, his breath a whisper against her skin.

Her heart thudded into a dangerous rhythm as she looked into the endless darkness of his eyes. They were mesmerizing, haunting, and as the heavy-lidded sensuality pulled her deeper and deeper she knew she was heading fast into something explosive. But it didn't matter. She didn't move, couldn't move, then he bent closer and kissed her.

CHAPTER TEN

HER MOUTH WAS EVEN SOFTER than he'd expected. Drawing her even closer, Cole pressed his lips against hers, a groan building inside him. She moved toward him or did he imagine it? Want it so badly that he just thought she was coming to him?

For one long moment, he didn't care either way. All he could think about was Taylor…the way she smelled, the way her eyes turned darker when she was thinking about something, how soft her skin felt beneath his fingers as they made their way slowly down her neck to the opening of her robe.

She murmured something, her lips moving under his. It almost sounded as if it were a protest but then she actually did come closer to him, one slender arm reaching out to loop around his neck and bring him toward her. He responded as any man would—he pressed his chest against hers, as his tongue outlined her lips then slipped between them to deepen the kiss.

They stayed that way for only seconds, then dimly, Cole realized Taylor was retreating from him. She didn't actually move away, but he sensed her withdrawal…maybe even before she knew it herself.

He drew back, reluctantly breaking the kiss and the embrace as her perfume rose between them, the natural scent of her skin, not any kind of expensive oils or lotions. Dazed with longing, her eyes took him in, the lids heavy with a desire that almost made him lose what little sense he had left.

He spoke first, with a husky whisper, almost unintelligible. "I'm a damned fool. If I had any brains at all, I'd take you back to town right this very minute."

She wet her lips. "But the roads are terrible—"

"And that's the only reason we're staying here." His eyes caressed her face a moment longer, studying the curves and planes, committing the feel of her skin to his memory. Then he rose abruptly to look down on her, his voice now as hard as his eyes. "So lock your door tonight, Taylor. I don't want to be making any more mistakes."

THE NEXT MORNING dawned frigid and silent. When Taylor opened her eyes and saw the white coating on the window outside she didn't know what was worse—the weather or what had happened between her and Cole.

What was she doing kissing another man the way she'd kissed Cole? Having feelings for another man as she was having for Cole? She'd promised Richard she'd be thinking about their relationship and instead she couldn't get Cole out of her mind. And he'd instantly regretted kissing her, she could tell from his expression. It was more than obvious he didn't want to care for her for whatever reason.

Moaning, she buried her face in the pillow and only the insistent aroma of freshly brewed coffee, wafting its way under the bedroom door, pulled her up. Making a grimace of disgust but having no other choice, she threw on the jeans and sweater she'd worn the day before, then went into the bathroom to wash her face and draw a comb through her hair. There was nothing else she could do. She had no makeup. No perfume. Nothing. Given the kiss they'd shared last night, she was almost glad. Another encounter similar to that would put everything in a very different perspective.

Not that it hadn't already.

There was a note beside the simmering coffeepot. He'd set out a clean mug and the sugar bowl.

Gone to check on the cattle. Be back in an hour. Eggs in the fridge if you want breakfast.

Both relieved and disappointed, Taylor poured a cup of coffee and drifted to the nearby window, disliking the feeling of isolation. Cole had obviously taken Lester with him, and she found herself missing the dog, not to mention the man. She stared out the glass. A light, almost invisible layer of something white—ice or snow, she couldn't tell which—covered the ground for as far as she could see. The early morning sun dazzled it, sending out diamonds of light so sharp she had to squint to see. The cold whiteness brought back memories of Montana, and for the first time in years, she thought about life in a small town in a positive way. Life where you could breathe the air, not taste it. Life where you could see the morning coming.

Turning away from the window, and from her memories as well, Taylor walked resolutely toward the phone on the kitchen wall. She dialed the motel. The bored operator gave her two messages, one from Jim Henderson, the other from Richard.

Taylor swallowed hard and put the receiver back in the cradle. Richard. Had he come home early? The number he'd left was the number of the office. He must have returned unexpectedly and Martha had been forced to tell him where she was. Now Taylor was going to have to explain.

And she had no idea how.

Postponing the inevitable, she called Jim first.

"Taylor! I'm so glad you called. How are you feeling?" The older man had concern in his voice. Cole had phoned him last night and told him she'd had a car accident but he hadn't gone into any more detail.

"I'm fine," she answered, "just a little sore. I really appreciate you calling Cole, though. I might still be out there if you hadn't."

"Well, for once I guess I'm glad I'm a nosy old man," he said with a laugh. "Thank goodness you were okay. You're very lucky the brakes didn't go out when you were nearer the edge."

"Yes, I am. But now we're stuck out at Cole's—

the bad weather may keep us here. I don't think I'll be able to see you today.''

"Well, I have great news so it's not even important we meet today. We got a call yesterday from a possible buyer. He's flying in tomorrow from Odessa to look at Diablo. He's looking for a place to raise some exotic game. A preserve of sorts. Could you and Cole go out there with us tomorrow if the roads clear up?''

Surprise rippled over her, surprise and some other emotion she couldn't quite identify. "Already? I'm shocked we got a call this fast.''

"Me, too. Keep your fingers crossed and maybe it'll work out.''

They agreed on a time to meet at Jim's office, then Taylor hung up. She should have been excited, elated even, but she wasn't. In fact, she felt more anxious than ever, a nagging sensation that wouldn't go away, but she couldn't say exactly why. She replayed Jim's words in her head, but found nothing in the conversation that should have made her feel that way. She decided it must just be nerves. She'd gone through such a roller-coaster ride lately. Actually selling Diablo had been only a dream for so long, maybe the reality, or at least the possibility, of seeing it go was more than she could handle at the moment. She put aside her confusing emotions and reluctantly picked up the phone again.

Thinking she'd get the details first, she asked for Martha when the receptionist answered.

"She's in with Mr. Williams, Mrs. Matthews. Shall I ring in there?"

Taylor grimaced, the phone suddenly slippery in her hand. "Uh, sure. That's fine."

He answered on the third ring, just as he always did.

"Richard Williams here."

Taylor's mouth went dry and she couldn't speak.

"Hello? Is anyone there?" His voice sounded curt and in a hurry—just the opposite of Cole's slow, sensual drawl.

"I-it's Taylor," she finally said. "Can you talk or are you busy?"

After a moment's pause, he spoke. "Oh, Taylor... Just a moment, please."

She could hear him put his hand over the phone and a muffled conversation taking place. A second later, he came back on, the sound of a door closing in the background. He sounded puzzled, almost hurt. "What are you doing out there, Taylor? I thought we agreed you weren't going to the ranch."

"That's not exactly how I remember it, Richard."

"We said we'd discuss the topic further. The next thing I know I come home and instead of finding you taking a vacation as I suggested, you're gone. Couldn't we have talked about this, sweetheart?"

"I wanted to, but...well, it seemed as if we weren't going to ever have the time so I made the decision on my own. I hope you're not mad, Richard."

"Mad? Of course, I'm not mad, but I *am* disappointed. I wanted to talk about the situation with you. That's all, darling."

Feeling guilty, she closed her eyes for a second, then reopened them. "You may not understand my motives, but they are good ones. And coming out here has only strengthened them."

"What are you saying?"

She started to explain, to tell him about everything that had happened, then for some inexplicable reason, she bit off the words, swallowing them instead of speaking them. "I'm still convinced that selling the place is what I should do—that's all I meant."

"Well, sweetheart, I think you're making a mistake, but it *is* your property. I guess I should butt out. I only wish you trusted my opinion more."

"Oh, Richard! It's not that. I just—"

"Then come home, darling." His tone turned conciliatory as he interrupted her. "Come home, wear my ring, and make me the happiest man in Houston. Forget about everything out there. It's not important."

"I can't do that, Richard, I'm sorry."

A tight tension-filled silence echoed down the line.

"What *exactly* is it you can't do?"

Just as Richard spoke, Taylor glanced out the frosted window and saw Cole coming toward the house from the barn, his boots kicking up the snow along the path into tiny puffs of white. He had on a long leather duster and his battered black hat, faded jeans tightly molding to his thighs and calves, denim straining as he took his usual strides forward, the coat flapping open with each lengthy step. Looking as intense as ever, his face was turned to the sky, studying it.

And suddenly she couldn't breathe. Or talk. Or think.

"Taylor?" Richard's concerned voice broke into the silence. "I'm waiting here. Which is it?"

"I have to go," she said.

"Excuse me?"

"I'm going to hang up now, Richard." She took a deep breath. "I'll call you later."

SHE WAS STANDING by the window when he walked inside. A single ray of sun was pouring through the glass, striking the side of her face and lighting her profile to show its stark perfection.

"I saw you coming," she said, a catch in her voice. Raising her hand she gestured vaguely toward the window. "It...looks cold outside."

"It is." He stood where he was, not bothering to take off his coat or hat, his eyes locked on her face. He'd stayed awake half the night thinking about their kiss, wanting to walk down the hall and turn the knob to his bedroom, wanting to step inside and spend the remaining hours making love to her.

But he'd done it only in his dreams.

"I—I just got off the phone with Jim Henderson. He has someone who wants to look at Diablo tomorrow."

"You don't sound too excited about it."

She raised one hand to the base of her neck, an uncertain touch of two fingers in the hollow there. He followed their movement with his eyes. "I—I am excited," she said, her gaze never leaving his.

"Good."

They just looked at each other, and he imagined he saw—reflected in the green depths of her eyes— his own thoughts of tangled sheets and overheated bodies.

Finally, she broke the moment. "How are the roads?"

He blinked, mentally shaking himself for being such a fool. "Fine. As soon as the sun came out, they were okay. We can leave now if you like."

"I'll get my purse."

She brushed past him, heading for the bedroom, and his hand shot out on its own, capturing her arm. She stopped abruptly and looked up at him. They were standing close enough for him to see a tiny mole near the corner of her right eyebrow. His mother would have called it a beauty mark. He wondered how it would feel beneath his lips.

"About last night…"

She stood silently.

"I'm sorry."

She blinked, a slow languid movement that made

her eyelashes brush against the ivory of her cheek before she looked up at him again. His heart sped up, especially when she licked her lips and spoke, the words so soft he could barely hear them.

"That's too bad," she whispered. "Because I'm not."

He stared at her, dumbfounded, then watched as she turned around and left the room. Had she really said the words or had he imagined them? Was his hearing playing tricks on him as his dreams had last night?

He wondered about it all the way to town.

But he didn't ask.

Pulling the truck up to the motel, he turned and looked at her, not knowing what to say. She took care of the situation for him.

"I'm meeting Jim Henderson and his client tomorrow afternoon at one. Do you think you could go with us? Jim said he wanted to show the man the canyon and I don't think I can find it."

Cole nodded. "I have a group arriving, but they'll need a while to settle in. I'll be there. At one."

Their eyes locked and something passed between them, something Cole wished he didn't understand and could just ignore...but knew he couldn't.

THE REST OF THE DAY passed in a blur for Taylor. After he dropped her off at the motel all she could think about was Cole and the kiss they'd shared. It'd been a long time—a very long time—since a man had made her feel that way.

Richard had never even come close.

Sighing, she closed her eyes and sank down onto the sagging mattress. Was she prepared to tell him it was over? She was really grateful for his support the past few years but was gratitude enough to sustain a relationship?

She leaned back against the pillows, closed her eyes and pretended she didn't know the answer.

She was nodding off when the phone woke her. Stumbling up from the beginning of a dream, she jumped from the bed and grabbed the receiver on the fifth ring.

"Mrs. Matthews?"

She recognized Sheriff Shipley's voice immediately and tensed. "Yes?"

"I'm calling about the little problem you had with your room the other night. I have a question for you."

"Yes?"

"I'm wondering if you saw a kid hanging around the motel. Brown hair, about five-nine or so, lightweight."

"I don't remember seeing anyone like that. Why? Is he a suspect?"

"I wouldn't call him that, but we want to ask him some questions. His name is Jody Jackson. One of the guests mentioned to my deputy that they'd seen someone fitting that description hanging around the motel the day before this happened. You don't know him?''

"No. I've never heard the name before. Who is he?''

"He's one of Teo Goodman's projects.'' His voice held derision. "Teo takes in kids from reservations across the country and tries to reform them. While he's teaching them to see the light, they usually manage to get into trouble. This one's worse than usual.''

"Why is that?''

"He's older and smarter than most of them. He's done graduate work in the criminal arena, courtesy of TDC.''

She frowned. "He's in college?''

The sheriff laughed. "Not hardly. I meant he'd been in the prison system already—the Texas Department of Corrections.''

"Oh, God...for what?''

"Just the usual. Drugs and attempted murder.''

Taylor abruptly sat back down on the bed. "Why would he be interested in me?''

"That's the missing part right now, especially since you don't know him. We're trying to talk to the rancher he works for, see if he knows anything.''

"Who would that be?''

"A guy named Cason. Owns a big spread called the Diamond C out west of town. He likes to think of himself as a local bigwig. He gives Teo's boys jobs now and then, working the cattle if they can ride or baling hay, stuff like that. I think Jackson works on his machinery. He learned to work on engines while he was in prison.''

Bob Hale's words sounded in Taylor's mind. *Some people around here aren't happy about your appearance in High Mountain…like the local ranchers for one.*

Her stomach knotted. ''And you're going to talk to Mr. Cason about this?''

''When he gets back. He's out of town. His wife says he's supposed to be back at the end of the week. He's buying cattle in Wyoming.''

Poised on the edge of the bed, Taylor listened numbly, then spoke. ''Do you think this kid destroyed my room at Cason's behest?''

''I'm not thinking anything yet, but I'll tell you this. Steven Cason is a very wealthy man. If he wanted you out of here, he'd buy you off. He wouldn't send some kid over to try and scare you away.''

''Are you sure?''

''I'm not sure of anything except God and taxes. But since you didn't think I was doing anything about your situation, I wanted to call and let you know otherwise. Jackson himself could be a complete dead end, and if he is, Cason's still not linked to any of this. Then again, you never know.''

''I think you should know something else happened, too.''

''I'm listening.''

She explained the accident the day before.

"Cole didn't look at the brakes?"

"We didn't have time. The storm was coming in and we had to get out of there."

"So it's possible the brakes just failed on their own?"

"It's possible but highly unlikely. I know you don't think much of my detecting skills, Sheriff, but I think even you are going to have admit it's looking as if some loony is after me."

A tense silence developed, then he spoke slowly and distinctly, as if the idea were just now coming to him. "'Some loony?' Do you mean someone with mental problems, Mrs. Matthews?" He paused expectantly, and for some reason, her pulse began to thud at the base of her neck. "Someone who, for example, has been in therapy for years? Someone like…yourself?"

Her mouth went dry. "I don't think I understand what you're implying, Sheriff."

"I've been doing a little checking of my own, Mrs. Matthews, and I learned something really interesting. Your husband had quite an insurance policy when he died and you were his sole beneficiary." He paused and went on. "Now you're back in High Mountain and spending time with Mr. Reynolds. If I was a suspicious man, I might wonder, wouldn't I?"

As if someone's fingers were suddenly around her neck Taylor's throat closed. Shocked, she couldn't catch her breath or speak, then finally she managed to draw a slow, incredulous breath. "Wh-what are you saying? That you think I engineered all these things myself?"

He didn't say anything.

"I hope I'm misunderstanding because that doesn't make any sense at all," she continued. "None."

"Stranger things have happened," he said finally.

"Well, not to me! For God's sake, we were both wounded. Do you actually think I'd shoot myself, then wound Cole, too? Or that I'd wait two years and come back here? I didn't even meet Cole Reynolds until Jack and I came to High Mountain!"

"Really?" His voice was hard.

"Yes, really. Your theory is ridiculous, Sheriff, and I'm insulted you'd even come up with it!"

"A million dollars can make people do crazy things, Mrs. Matthews. I know plenty of men who'd do worse for less. You and Mr. Reynolds *were* the only witnesses. Could be you even planned it together, then something went wrong and you both got hurt. Now you're back to even up the score and you want to look like the innocent victim while you're doing that."

"I loved my husband!" she said tightly.

"Maybe...but you also benefitted from his death."

"I didn't even know he had that insurance policy until after he died."

"He didn't tell you about a million-dollar policy?"

"My husband didn't tell me everything, Sheriff." She took a deep breath and tried to calm down, but it was almost impossible. She felt as though she had just fallen fifty feet. "This is insane. I've never heard of anything so absolutely crazy in my whole life."

"Crazy people do crazy things." She heard his chair creak, then he spoke again. "I'll be in touch, Mrs. Matthews. Don't leave town without letting me know."

CHAPTER ELEVEN

TAYLOR STEWED on the sheriff's words until she felt she was about to explode. The next day, as she waited for Cole outside Jim Henderson's office, she didn't feel any better. She and Cole planning Jack's murder? The thought of it made her sick.

Precisely at one o'clock, Cole's battered truck turned down Main Street and headed toward her. When she saw it coming, Taylor felt a sudden surge of hope. Cole would know what to do with Shipley's outrageous comments. He'd help her muddle through this. She wasn't completely alone.

He stepped out of the truck into the harsh winter sunlight. His face was shadowed by his well-worn hat, but Taylor didn't need to see his eyes to know he was staring at her. She could feel the heat of his gaze even though they were separated by at least fifty feet, and her heart did a funny flip that she felt all the way down to her toes.

She waited impatiently for him to cross the street. When he reached her side, she pulled him down to the bench where she'd been sitting and recounted the entire bizarre conversation. When she finished, he sat quietly.

"Well, say something," she sputtered. "Don't you think this is ridiculous?"

"Of course it's ridiculous," he said, his dark eyes flashing hotly. "But J. C. Shipley is not an idiot. He's run this county for a hundred years and he's done it by keeping his cards tight to his chest. He must have had a good reason for saying what he did."

"A good reason? There was *no* reason for him to say any of those things and you know it."

"Maybe he just wanted to start you thinking. Maybe he wanted to get you riled up. Maybe he's just throwing out lines, seeing what he can hook. At least he's working on the case again."

"But with wild theories like that, what are the chances he'll find the real killer?"

"Let him do it his way. He might surprise you."

She looked into Cole's eyes. Things in High Mountain hadn't been what they seemed so far. Maybe he had a point. "All right...but just so you know, I'm not planning on letting this drop."

"I didn't think you would," Cole answered, his voice dry.

The door to Jim's office opened a second later, and Jim walked out, a much younger man following behind him. Dressed in crisp, ironed jeans and a spotless parka, he smiled shyly in Cole's direction then tipped his hat toward Taylor as Jim introduced them all. "Taylor, this is Nate Freeman, the client I told you about."

Taylor rose and shook the young man's hand. He didn't seem old enough to have the kind of money needed to buy Diablo, but obviously he did or Jim wouldn't be bothering with him. "Nice to meet you, Mr. Freeman."

He smiled. "Call me Nate."

They piled into Jim's Range Rover, Jim and Nate in the front seat, Cole and Taylor in the back, and headed out of town. The conversation was light, but Taylor couldn't concentrate. Shipley's accusations stayed in her mind, worrying her like a rock in her shoe. Cole's reaction hadn't been what she'd expected. Did nothing rile the man? How could he look so hot and be so cool?

As if he had sensed her thoughts, Cole turned and trained his eyes on her. His stare was so intense she felt as though he were inside her head, reading her mind like a well-thumbed book.

"Forget Shipley." He spoke so quietly Jim never stopped talking to Nate. "You're making a big deal out of nothing."

She started to protest, but suddenly she knew he was right. Staring out the window, all Taylor could do was ask herself why. Why did she care if the sheriff thought she and Cole had done something wrong? Why?

She already felt guilty, that's why, and the sheriff's illogical words had triggered an even deeper avalanche of the emotion. She *was* attracted to Cole—in the very worst sort of way—and she was going to have to call Richard and tell him the truth. Tell him she couldn't marry him.

Nate Freeman's soft voice broke into her convoluted thoughts. "So sorry about the circumstances of the sale and your husband's death."

Taylor forced herself into the present to acknowledge the young man's words. "Thank you, Nate, that's very kind of you. I hope you won't let the accident influence what you think of Diablo, though. It's a gorgeous place."

They reached the edge of town and then the cutoff to the ranch a half hour later. Jim pulled the huge truck up to the cattle guard then stopped. Looking over his shoulder at Cole, he spoke. "I'd appreciate it if you'd explain the terrain to Nate, Cole. You know this area a lot better than I do."

"No problem. I'd be happy to."

Jim nodded then maneuvered the vehicle over the guard as Cole leaned over the front seat and began to point out to Nate the features of the land. Tilting his head toward a stand of cedars, he showed them where the white-tailed deer gathered in the evening, then as they went on, he nodded toward the trails etched into the hard ground that revealed the path of the javelinas. Taylor found herself interested even though she didn't want to be. They drove in as far as they could, which was a lot closer to the canyon than most trucks could get them, then walked in the rest of the way.

When they reached the chasm, Taylor hung back.

Jim and Nate Freeman kept going toward the gaping edge. The air was so cold and crisp Taylor could almost taste it, the sky overhead a crystal kind of blue. Watching the two men walk away, Taylor tried to read Nate Freeman's mood but found it impossible. Strangely enough, she wasn't sure if she wanted him to love Diablo or hate it.

Cole came up to where she stood, leaning against a mesquite tree.

"I went by the old house this morning," he said, his eyes studying the horizon. "Checked out the Blazer."

Her heart suddenly in her throat, Taylor looked at Cole expectantly.

"I couldn't tell, Taylor, I'm sorry. The brake line was damaged when you started down the incline. There's no way to know what really happened."

"Great," she said in a disgusted voice. "Shipley will think I just rammed the truck into the tree." Something clicked in the back of her mind as soon as she said the words. She turned to Cole, sudden excitement in her voice. "But that Jackson kid— he's a mechanic. He would have known how to mess with the brakes, right?"

Cole frowned. "What are you talking about?"

"Jody Jackson—"

"What's he got to do with this?"

She realized in her anger she'd forgotten to tell him everything Shipley had said. She explained quickly. "Do you know him? This kid, I mean?"

"Yeah, I know him. Teo tried to get me to hire him when he first came to High Mountain but I declined."

"Why?"

"I didn't like the way he looked." She expected him to say more, but he didn't. His eyes narrowed into slits against the bright sunlight. "I wonder if Teo knows about this."

"I don't know. Shipley didn't say if he'd spoken to him or not."

Cole hit his hat against his leg and looked out into the distance. "Shipley wouldn't have to *tell* Teo for him to *know*." He glanced down at her. "My brother's an activist. He makes it his business to know everything."

"Could you call him and ask him about the kid?"

He raised one dark eyebrow. "Don't you want to give Shipley a chance to do his job?"

"He didn't two years ago. Why would he now?"

Cole met her steady gaze with a measuring one of his own, but before he could say anything, Jim and Nate walked back from the edge. Taylor and Cole joined them and they all headed toward the truck. After a moment, Taylor turned to the younger man. "So what do you think? Pretty spectacular, huh?"

He nodded slowly. "It *is* incredible. Plenty of space, natural boundaries, good grazing areas. I think the habitat would be perfect for the game I'm considering." His expression turned thoughtful.

"It's farther out of town than I'd expected, though. I'd be interested in seeing the old ranch house Jim mentioned. I'd need some quick overnight space for the construction workers while they're working on the property."

"Construction workers?" Taylor glanced at Jim then her eyes went back to Nate as they continued walking. "I thought you were just interested in a game preserve."

"That's right—exotic game—but we don't just put the animals out here and let 'em eat." He smiled. "We bring in tourists...and hunters when we need to. For the rates we're going to charge, people will expect nice rooms, luxurious even. I'll have to build them."

If the locals knew about these plans, she'd be in more trouble than she was already. Taylor nodded slowly, then cut her eyes to Cole's face to get his reaction to the news. They'd made their way back to the Rover and were standing beside it. He hadn't heard their exchange, though. He was stone-still and his expression was curious—poised and frozen—almost as if he heard something the rest of them couldn't. She stopped and listened herself, the faintest of sounds catching her attention. A ring of metal against metal? The quiet slap of a horse's tail?

Taylor reached for Cole without thinking. Her fingers found the soft sleeve of his coat and wrapped themselves around his arm. The leather was cold, and beneath her touch, the muscles were hard. He didn't move except to put his hand over hers. The heat of his touch brought an even deeper awareness to her, all her senses suddenly heightened, sharpened somehow.

And then she heard the sound again. A jingling. A rattle. She pulled her breath in sharply but it couldn't hold back the wave of dizziness that swept over her, bringing with it a realization as pointed as a knife blade held to her throat. She'd heard this sound before. Once in reality, then time and time again in her dreams, not knowing why, not understanding, the haunting ring of metal and leather.

And now she understood. Understood with a nauseating, overpowering clarity.

This was the sound she'd heard just before she'd been shot. Just before Jack had been killed. The distant sound of a horse's halter and...

She felt the blood drain from her face and her fingers tightened convulsively against Cole's arm. She opened her mouth to warn them, then the final *click*—the sound of a rifle's action pulling back— echoed in the deadly silence.

THE SHOT SOUNDED and Cole went down, pulling Taylor with him, rolling on top of her the minute they hit the bloodred dirt. Her scream ripped the silence and with an immediacy that stole his breath, Cole traveled two years back.

He raised his head and stared at her. "Are you okay? Were you hit?"

She didn't answer, her eyes two pieces of frozen green. Cole felt his heart trip against his chest. He grabbed her shoulders and shook them gently. "Are you okay?"

Blinking, she seemed to come back into herself. "Y-yes. Yes. I'm fine. Are you—"

"I'm okay."

Together they raised their heads and looked over where Jim and Nate had been standing. Both men were in the dirt, under the rear wheel well of the truck.

"Jim—you guys all right?"

A muffled answer came back. "Yeah, we're fine. Was that a rifle?"

"Yeah." Cole stared into the distance. "Stay down till I can tell what's going on. You don't have a weapon in the truck, do you?"

"There's a .22 under the backseat," he said apologetically. "But that's it."

Cole cursed under his breath. A .22 was useless out here. He'd almost be better off with a straw and a spitball. Before he'd left his house this morning, he'd thought about bringing his own rifle, had even put it in his truck, but when he'd seen Taylor sitting on the bench outside Jim's office looking as if the world had just ended, he'd forgotten the gun. Had walked off without it.

Obviously a very bad move.

Turning her head beneath him, Taylor spoke, her voice an urgent whisper. "Can you see anything?"

"No. Not a thing." His eyes searched the horizon for movement, for any fleck of action, but everything was still and quiet. "They could be a half mile away, though."

"And the shot came that close?"

"With a high-powered rifle, sure."

Her voice was hollow, distant. "It went right by my ear. Another inch and—" She started to tremble beneath him.

"It's okay, it's okay." Cradling her head with his hand, he steadied her, looking into her eyes. "Listen to me—you're all right, Taylor, okay?"

She shuddered, but managed to nod her head.

"I'm going to crawl to the door and open it. The minute it's wide enough, I want you to jump inside. You'll be better protected."

A second later, he was moving, and almost instantly he was beside the door. He reached up and opened it, then fell back to the ground. Almost before he was prostrate, Taylor was inside and on the floorboard. He called to Jim and Nate and they followed quickly. With one last look around, Cole jumped inside himself, started the engine and turned the truck, to head back the way they'd come. He didn't want to give the shooters any more of a profile than he had to, so he stayed low in the seat and gunned it, fully expecting more shots but never hearing them.

A single minute later, they were a mile away.

He glanced across the seat at Taylor. Her face was

ivory, completely without color. She'd knit her fingers together in her lap but they were trembling anyway. The graceful column of her throat jerked as she swallowed convulsively. They were almost to the main road, so he reached over and touched her leg. "Do you want me to stop?"

Her eyes were enormous as she glanced toward him and nodded. He barely had the truck halted before she yanked open the door. Running a few steps away, she began to retch. A few minutes later she came back into the vehicle, her face a sickening shade of celadon now.

No one said anything until they were almost to town.

Nate Freeman finally broke the silence, his voice shaky but determined. Taylor turned around to look at him. "Diablo's a beautiful place, Mrs. Matthews, but you've got problems that I don't need. I'm sure you understand—I can't take paying customers somewhere like that. It's a disaster waiting to happen."

"But it's me," she protested. "It's not the ranch—"

"Not to be disrespectful, ma'am, but how do you know that for sure? There's been lots of trouble out there."

They pulled up in front of Jim's office. Cole looked over in time to see Taylor biting her lip. She started to speak, but Nate Freeman already had the back door open and was climbing out. He tipped his hat. "Best of luck to you, Mrs. Matthews. I think you're going to need it."

Cole, Taylor and Jim watched as the young man crossed the street and climbed inside a rented red Bronco. He left without a backward glance and the three of them climbed out of the Rover and stood in front of the office.

Jim turned to Taylor, an apologetic but guarded expression on his still pale face. "I can't take clients out there again, Taylor, not like this. I know this wasn't your fault but until we find out what's going on, it's just not safe."

"I know, Jim. I—I don't know what to do about this."

"There's nothing for *you* to do," Cole said. When Taylor's scared gaze touched his, he almost wished she hadn't turned. His stomach knotted in a delayed reaction and he felt as if he'd be the next one throwing up. What exactly would he have done if she'd been hit? Again? He couldn't let himself think about it. He spoke instead. "We're going down to the sheriff's office right now. This is his problem."

"That's pointless—"

"You don't have another option, Taylor, and whether it's pointless or not, we've got to let the man know. This wasn't an accident, and there's no way he can blow it off and say you were involved." He looked up the street, then back down at her, his throat closing with the possibility of what could have been. "Let's go, Taylor. Right now."

She hesitated for only a second, then she turned and gave Jim a quick kiss. "I'll be in touch, okay?"

"That's fine, honey. You just let me know what's going on...and take care, all right?"

"I will."

Cole was already going up the sidewalk by the time she caught up with him. Wordlessly they crossed the street and headed in the direction of the sheriff's office. He was sitting behind his desk and his expression didn't change as Taylor explained the situation.

He looked at Cole when she finished. "You were there?"

"Standing right beside her." Cole stared at the man from the other side of his desk. "You've got to do something. Taylor was almost killed, J.C."

He looked alarmed. "The shot came that close?"

Cole nodded. Taylor abruptly sat down in one of the chairs in front of the desk, her face pale as she closed her eyes. Cole walked over to her and gently put his hand on her neck, forcing her head down to keep her from fainting.

"Phone calls and sliced tires are one thing. Even the accident with the truck could be explained but this?" Cole shook his head. "Another inch and we'd be having a much different discussion. You need to look into this. Right now."

The two men stared at each other. Although he didn't like Shipley, Cole had defended him to Taylor—the man had been around for too long to be too crooked—but Cole read something he didn't like in the other man's small narrow eyes. Did Shipley have some vested interest in this?

Their eyes held for a moment, then Shipley looked away. "I'll get on it," he said, shuffling with the papers on his desk that suddenly claimed his attention. "Soon as possible. Give Joe a statement on your way out."

An hour later, they walked out of the office, then stopped on the sidewalk, Taylor halting just outside the door. She turned her face to Cole's, and her look made something turn inside him.

"Shipley's not going to do a thing with this. It's up to me." She glanced at the office before she looked back at Cole, grim determination coming over her expression. "You said your brother knows everything that goes on in this town. Well, I want to talk to him. Will you take me to him?"

Cole thought of the pottery fragment. "You don't want Teo involved in this, Taylor."

"But he knows the Jackson kid! And he might be able to help us."

"Teo helps himself, not other people."

She crossed her arms and stared at him. "What is it with you two? Why are you so angry at him?"

He couldn't think of a way to explain, so Cole simply turned and started to walk away. Taylor stopped him, her hand on his arm.

"Cole? Tell me, please. I want to know."

He stared at her, then found himself reaching up

to touch a smudge of red dust clinging to her cheek. Beneath his finger, her skin felt like glass—smooth, cold, fragile.

She took his hand in hers and held it. "I want to know," she said quietly.

"It's not important."

"Then why are you lying about it?"

Their eyes fastened on each other, and Cole felt himself drowning. "Go clean up," he said roughly. "I'll pick you up outside the motel in an hour. We'll get something to eat."

SHE TOOK A HOT SHOWER and washed the red dirt out of her hair but nothing could wash away the sound of the shot whizzing by her ear. Taylor shook her head every time she thought about it and forced herself to focus on getting ready instead. Taking a clean pair of jeans and a bulky green sweater from the closet, she slipped into them then dabbed on a little lipstick and mascara. As the numbers on the clock radio audibly flipped to the hour, she heard Cole's truck pull into the parking lot.

She ran to the door, thrusting her arm into the sleeve of her coat as she went. Her ring caught on the lining, though, and a loud rip echoed in the room.

She stopped and cursed, and when she pulled her arm back out, part of the lining came with it. The stone winked coldly up at her. She looked at it for a moment, then she took off the ring and laid it on the table beside her bed, and walked out the door without the coat or the diamond.

It was chilly inside the truck, but under Cole's hot gaze she barely noticed.

"Where's your coat?" Not waiting for an answer, he handed her his leather jacket. "Here, put this on." She nodded and took the garment from him to slip over her shoulders. She fought the urge to bury her nose in the collar and satisfied herself with taking a deep, pulling breath. Smoky fires. Warm beds.

"I thought we might drive over to Lajitas—have Mexican food for dinner. That all right with you?"

She glanced across the cab. His profile was sharp in the dim lights from the dash. "Lajitas? Isn't that down by the border?"

He nodded. "It'll just take an hour or so to get there. It's only about eighty miles from High Mountain."

"Sure, why not?" She laughed, pulling the coat closer. "I guess that's the same as running to the corner store in Houston, huh?"

"When you have to ride five miles of fence post to see your nearest neighbor, you don't mind going eighty miles for enchiladas." He glanced across the seat and smiled. "They're really good enchiladas, too."

He seemed to sense that she didn't want to talk about the shooting. So they talked of other things, the black miles going by quickly, the ghostly range a blur in the endless dark beside the road. By the time they reached the diner, she had almost lost the sharp edge of fear that had been with her since they'd gone to Diablo.

He opened the door of the dimly lit bar and held it for her. "It looks pretty bad," Cole warned her. "But the food's great."

He was right. On both accounts.

After they finished their meal, the waitress brought them *cafe con leche* and a small bowl of cinnamon with a tiny spoon. Taylor watched Cole sprinkle the cinnamon on top of his coffee and knew she'd never smell it again without thinking about this very moment. He looked up, his dark eyes piercing, even in the gloom of the booth where they sat.

His stare was almost too much. She leaned back against the red leather and sought the pockets of his jacket with her trembling hands. Instantly, something sharp scratched the edge of her thumb. She gingerly wrapped her fingers around the object and pulled her hand out. In her grasp was a piece of something hard and black, white lines scratched across the surface in a pattern that looked strangely familiar even though she couldn't place it. A single drop of her blood glistened on the edge. She looked up at Cole. "What on earth is this? I cut myself on it."

He cursed and reached for her hand. Dipping his napkin in a nearby glass of water he gently cleaned the cut, holding her fingers between his. "God, I forgot about that. I'm sorry."

She watched him, her heart moving up from her chest into the vicinity of her throat, making it difficult to speak. "I-it's nothing."

He wrapped her finger and kept pressure on it with his own. She sat perfectly still and he reached across the table with his other hand, picking up the object, his eyes taking on a strange, glittery brightness.

Finally his eyes met hers above the table. "This is a piece of Jumano pottery," he said reluctantly. "I found it out at Diablo."

"It's beautiful."

"Yes, it is." He hesitated, then took a deep breath and spoke. "And it's the main reason you can't go to Teo and ask him for help. If he knows about this, he'll make so much trouble for you that the problems you've had so far will seem like minor irritations." His expression went grim. "My brother will make your life miserable."

"Why would he do that?"

"For one thing, he just likes to raise hell, but also because he's the head of the local Indian Council and he's rabid about preserving Jumano heritage. If he knew I'd found this at Diablo, he'd get an injunction against you so fast your head would spin. You'd never be able to sell the ranch. It'd be tied up in the courts forever while he tried to protect it."

"Is this kind of pottery rare?"

"Very. Usually it's a sign of burial fields."

"So he would definitely be against any construction in the area."

"Absolutely."

"But it's not his land."

"Prior claim doesn't matter to Teo."

His voice was so bitter and angry, Taylor flinched. "You sound as if this has happened before."

He raised his gaze from the shard and she was shocked by the expression in his eyes. Never had she seen them so cold, so remote. Behind the distance, though, flames of hatred shimmered, flames so intense, Taylor found herself shrinking away from him.

"My brother thinks of no one but himself. He takes what he wants, Taylor, and he doesn't care who gets hurt. Stay away from him. As far away as you can."

CHAPTER TWELVE

TAYLOR STARED AT HIM a moment longer, confusion making its way across her face before it cleared and she accepted his words. She reached across the table and took his hands in hers. "All right," she said quietly. "I'll stay away from him…but on one condition."

"And that is?"

"You talk to him for me. Ask him about Jody Jackson and find out where he was the night my motel room was torn up. Ask him about Steve Cason and whether or not he'd want me out of town. You don't have to say anything about the pottery. It's not related to any of this."

Cole wanted to refuse, even opened his mouth to say no, but her eyes were too green, her skin too pale, her oval face already etched too deeply into his mind to refuse her anything. "All right," he said reluctantly, "but he probably won't tell me anything."

"Just try," she said. "That's all I'm asking."

They left a few minutes after that, Cole's hand fitting perfectly into the hollow of Taylor's back as he directed her out of the bar and into the freezing night. Their footsteps crunched as they walked out to the truck, bright light from a full moon paving the area with silver. She brushed past him as he opened the truck door, and once she climbed inside, he closed it and walked to his side of the vehicle, telling himself he'd drop her off at the motel and not even get out of the truck.

But of course, that wasn't how it went.

When they pulled into the motel's parking lot, Taylor turned to him in the darkness. He couldn't see her expression. "Would you like to come inside? For a nightcap?"

A second later they were heading to her room. Cole knew he was making an enormous mistake even as he stepped through the door and entered the tiny space, dominated by a huge bed. He stopped, but she'd taken off his coat and was opening the minibar, soft light from a nearby lamp picking out the golden highlights from her hair and softening the fatigue in her features. She looked up at him and spoke. "Coke? Jack Daniel's? Wine?"

With a doomed feeling, he answered, "I'll take the Jack."

She nodded. "Sit down. Make yourself more comfortable."

He didn't bother. Nothing would make him comfortable, except bringing her into his arms and kissing her.

She brought him his drink, the ice cubes clinking against the side of the plastic glass. "I hope it's all

right,'' she said with a smile. "I'm not much of a
bartender—''

With his eyes never leaving her face, Cole took
the drink and set it down on the table beside him.
He couldn't stop himself. He pulled her into his
arms.

Her startled eyes met his.

"Kiss me," he said, his voice a husky plea. "So
I'll know that first time was just a fluke. That it
couldn't possibly have been as good as I keep remembering it."

Her hands were on his chest, flattened against his
sweater. Beneath the wool, he could feel their
warmth and he couldn't help but wonder how warm
the rest of her body was as well.

Raising her eyes to his, the shadow of her lashes
brushed over her cheeks. "I'm not sure that's a good
idea," she said slowly.

"I *know* it isn't," he answered, "but I don't give
a damn right now. I just want to kiss you."

She nodded slowly. Then she raised her hands to
either side of his face and cradled his jaw, her fingers tracing a line of fire. Touching him like this,
she closed her eyes, as if she wanted to somehow
file away the memory without an image to go with
it. After a second, she moved closer to him and drew
his head to hers.

Their lips met. Slowly, gently, almost tentatively,
they kissed, then something seemed to ignite inside
Cole's chest and he wrapped his arms around her,

crushing her to him. She murmured beneath the on-
slaught but it wasn't a protest. Meeting his desire
with an equal need, Taylor opened her mouth to his,
her small tongue going inside his mouth with quick,
urgent darts.

His hands slipped down her back to cup the sweet
curve of her buttocks, but after a moment's caress,
the touch only made him want more. He slid his
fingers upward, to the edge of her sweater, then went
beneath it to the soft, warm skin he'd expected. A
groan built deep inside him and he let the sound
rumble through him, a measure of his immeasurable
desire for her.

She answered him by doing the same. By easing
her own hands beneath the sweater he wore to dance
across his bare chest, to feel his skin, to caress each
inch that she could find. And before he could be
surprised, she lifted the heavy wool, her lips seeking
the places her hands had just been, her mouth moving from one spot to another and leaving a trail of
fiery kisses that only added to his upheaval, especially when they found his nipples and she laved
them with her tongue.

He stepped back, taking her with him, and moved
them both to the bed, raising her sweater over her
head as they reached the edge of the mattress. A
white lacy bra teased him as he sat down, Taylor
standing captured between his knees with nowhere
to go, her breasts filling his eyes and then his hands
as he nuzzled his face against her chest. Letting her

head fall back, she groaned, his lips and tongue teasing her nipples, the lace no barrier to the need building between them.

It took a moment for him to realize the phone was ringing.

"Ignore it," he said, his steady gaze meeting her startled one.

"I can't."

"Sure you can. I do it all the time."

"But it might be important."

"More important than this?"

She hesitated a second more, then stepped away from him and picked up the phone. When she spoke, after a moment's listening, her voice was thick. "I— I can't talk right now."

Cole could hear the voice on the other end. Masculine. Authoritative.

Taylor gripped the phone and shook her head. "I said I can't talk. I'll try and call you later." The voice was still speaking when she hung up the phone and turned back to Cole.

"Richard?"

She nodded.

He rose slowly from the bed and picked up his sweater. Yanking it over his head, he grabbed the drink she'd poured him earlier, then downed it in one gulp and turned back to face her, the liquor burning inside him, replacing the desire with a faint echo of what could have been.

"Are you leaving?"

"Yes. And it's just as well. I would have stopped it anyway."

She started to protest. "But, Cole, I—"

He walked up to where she stood and cupped her face with his hand. Looking into her eyes, he shook his head. "I won't make love to another man's woman. And I won't take her away from him when she isn't thinking straight."

"But I *am* thinking straight. Look!" She turned and pointed to the nightstand. "See the ring? I took it off before I went to dinner."

His heart took a sudden jump, but he forced it back down and shook his head. "That doesn't mean a thing, Taylor," he said softly. "Until you tell the man the truth, he's going to assume you're promised to him. And I can't let you betray that trust. It'd poison our relationship even before it *became* a relationship, and things would never, ever be the same between us. You'd end up hating me, and I would hate myself, too." He smiled gently and rubbed his thumb over the delicate line of her jaw. "I know what I'm talking about. Trust me."

He leaned down and kissed her, then turned and left. When he reached his truck, it was snowing.

TAYLOR GOT INTO BED but her sleep was so restless, she would have been better off simply staying awake. She kept remembering the feel of Cole's fingers on her back, the warmth of his mouth on her skin. At 3 a.m., exhausted and completely wrung

out, she fell into a state somewhere between awareness and dreaming, and that was almost worse. She
kept waking up and realizing her dreams were just
that—only dreams. By six, she gave up, rising from
the tangled sheets and rumpled pillows to stand beside the window. The moon was still out, limning
the parking lot with light, while on the other side of
the horizon, a single ribbon of pale peach was just
beginning to rise above the horizon.

Cole was right. She had to call Richard and tell
him. Tell him it was all over. Tell him she couldn't
wear his ring. It wasn't fair to let him think things
were going to work out between them when they
never would. The feelings she was having now for
Cole made any kind of relationship between her and
Richard impossible, to say the least.

But the thought of picking up the phone and dial-
ing Richard's number was too much to bear. She'd
almost rather face that whizzing bullet again. He'd
done so much for her, had helped her so much…and
this was how she was repaying him. She was going
to break his heart.

She looked out the window, her fingers pressed
against the cold, wet glass, the distant mountains a
blur of dark purple shadows.

Richard deserved better. The least she could do
was tell him in person. She would go back to Houston and face him, explain everything to him and
suffer the look that would come into his eyes.

Once the decision was made, she felt better. She

took a shower, then picked out a pair of black leggings and an oversize ivory sweater from the clothes she'd bought after her room had been destroyed. By 8 a.m., she was heading out the door. She'd have to find another rental car and make her airline reservations. She'd booked the motel room for an indefinite stay, too, so she'd need to tell them she was checking out. First she'd have breakfast, then she'd tend to all the details.

Walking briskly toward the diner, Taylor was almost past the local art gallery when her mind registered what her eyes had just seen. She stopped abruptly and retraced her steps, her gloved hand touching the window of the gallery as if she wanted to make sure of what she was seeing.

In the window, a tiny black pot stood on a pedestal, light shining on its glossy surface. Nothing else was in the display, but nothing else was needed. The six-inch-high vase, with its graceful slim neck and thicker, rounded body was stunning in its shape and design. A single motif, a white zigzagged line, circled its circumference. The arresting simplicity of the piece struck her, and suddenly she understood something she never had before—the seemingly endless parade of people who came into Jack's gallery with their checkbooks in their hands and no other thought in their minds except to possess what they were looking at.

She stepped to the door of the gallery and tried the doorknob, but it was still too early. The door was locked. Unexpected disappointment came over her. She stood in front of the window a moment longer, then reluctantly left to eat breakfast.

In twenty minutes, she was back.

As the bell over the door sounded softly, a woman emerged from the back of the store and greeted Taylor. Obviously in charge, she was tall, close to six feet, Taylor guessed, with a long braid of silver hair wrapped around her head. She wore a broomstick skirt of light purple fabric and a matching vest of the same shade. The color highlighted her pale blue eyes set in an already striking face. "May I help you?"

Taylor smiled and tilted her head to the piece in the window. "I had to come in and ask you about that. It's gorgeous."

The woman returned Taylor's smile. "It is beautiful, isn't it? If only it were authentic!"

"It's a reproduction?"

"Yes." The woman moved toward the pot and picked it up, cradling it in her fingers a moment before handing it over to Taylor. "I wouldn't be allowed to sell it if it weren't. It's illegal to sell Jumano pottery without permission from the local Indian council."

Taylor took the vase, the fired ceramic cool and smooth beneath her fingers. Turning it over, she marveled at the exquisite beauty.

"It is an exact reproduction, however, and has been certified as such." The saleswoman's expression was almost apologetic. "That's why it's so expensive."

Taylor nodded, glancing at the four-figure price tag. "How much would a real one cost?"

"I'm not even sure, it's been so long since I've had one." She crossed her arms in front of her chest in a disapproving gesture. "I was offered a piece a few years ago, but I didn't take it since it hadn't been approved for sale. They wanted almost thirty thousand for it." She shrugged. "I get so few tourists in here, I couldn't have bought it anyway. The best I could have done was arrange for a gallery to bid on it. Maybe in Sante Fe or Taos."

"What kind of shape was it in?"

"Not too good, actually. But they're so rare, it wouldn't have mattered." She looked at Taylor closely. "You know the right questions to ask. Are you in the business?"

Taylor looked up from the pot. "My husband was. I'm Taylor Matthews. I own—"

"Diablo, of course. I'm Patricia Brown. Nice to meet you, Mrs. Matthews. I have to say I'm surprised you're interested in that, though." She nodded toward the pot. "I had heard you were selling the ranch, couldn't wait to get out of here. Are you interested in our local culture?"

"Who wouldn't be interested in something this lovely?" Taylor held up the pot to the sunshine pouring in the window, then she handed it back to the gallery owner. "Wrap it up," she said impulsively, "I just can't leave without it."

"That's the best kind of piece to have," the woman said with a smile. "You won't be sorry."

SNOW STILL DUSTED the piñon trees outside when Cole pulled up to the small, squat building that housed the Indian Council. A collection of older, beatup trucks and cars decorated the parking lot, and to one side a little boy was playing with a yellow mutt, throwing a stick and laughing as the dog grabbed it and ran the other way. Sitting in his truck, listening to the engine cool off and tick down, Cole flashed back to his first dog. He'd rescued it from the pound, then lied to his mother and said he was only keeping it for a friend. Just a few days, he'd told her, figuring he could dream up another lie when his time ran out.

Teo had told on him and his mother had insisted Cole return the animal. He'd been crushed and Teo had been rewarded for telling the truth.

Climbing out of the vehicle and into the biting wind, Cole wondered what he was doing here. He'd promised Taylor, of course, but why? Teo wasn't going to help them. He didn't help anyone if it didn't help him, too.

Cole pushed the door open and stepped inside the bleak little office. Two metal desks were lined up against one wall, a row of plastic chairs waiting against the other. Above the chairs, there were sev-

eral blown-up photos of his brother with various
people, some Cole recognized, some he didn't. Most
of them were handing Teo checks. On the other side
of the room, someone had taped up a couple of
travel posters, but nothing could disguise the hopeless feel of the tiny office. Disappointment had
seeped into the walls and furniture. The council's
secretary, a skinny, disinterested woman, barely
looked up as Cole entered.

He stood beside her desk. "Is my brother in?"

She tilted her head lethargically to indicate the
inner office. "They're back there."

Cole crossed the small space then knocked once
on the plywood door. Without waiting for an answer, he opened it and stepped inside.

Then wished he hadn't.

Teo was sitting behind his desk and standing by
his side, leaning over to look at a file, was Beryl.
Her eyes widened as she took in Cole's appearance,
and she straightened up slowly, one hand at her
throat.

She was as beautiful as ever. Tall and slender,
ribbons of dark hair hanging down on either side of
a classic oval face. Almond eyes, black as midnight.

Cole stared at her and waited for his heart to do
something. To ache and burn. To knock against his
chest. To break slowly.

But it did none of those things. It just kept on
beating, slowly but reliably, just as it should. He was
shocked—and relieved—until he realized his reac-

tion, or lack thereof, probably had something to do with Taylor. And that scared him even more.

He nodded in Beryl's direction then looked at his brother. Wearing a smirk, Teo reached over lazily and put his hand around Beryl's waist. "Hey, little brother. What are you doing here?"

"I came to talk to you," Cole answered, his eyes never leaving Teo's face. "About one of your kids."

"Have a seat." Teo waved toward one of the plastic chairs in front of his desk. "Are you finally realizing you should help us out? Are you going to hire someone?"

Cole sat down and balanced his hat on his knee. He was vaguely aware of Beryl's stare, but he didn't want to look at her, didn't want to give his heart a second chance to react just in case it was fooling him. "I'm not here to hire anyone, Teo. I just want some information. About Jody Jackson."

There was a flicker of something in Teo's eyes. Cole wouldn't have seen it if he hadn't been concentrating so hard on not looking at Beryl. Even so, he couldn't tell exactly what it was he'd just seen in his brother's expression. Confusion? Concern?

Teo nodded. "Jody Jackson. He works for Steve Cason. I don't think Steve would turn loose of him—"

"I'm not here for that," Cole interrupted. "I want to know what you know about him."

"Why?"

"Taylor's had a few problems over at the motel

and Shipley told her someone saw a kid who looked like Jody hanging around there.''

"So it's 'Taylor' now? What happened to 'Mrs. Matthews'?''

Beryl turned away from the desk to busy herself at the small computer in one corner of the office. She had her back to them, her slim, slightly curved back, which Cole had had memorized at one time.

Cole ignored Teo's taunt. "Is he still with Cason?''

"As far as I know.'' Teo leaned toward his desk and put his elbows on the corner, his eyes narrowing. "So Shipley's spreading rumors, then?'' Without waiting for Cole's answer, Teo spoke again. "Our esteemed sheriff is sticking his nose where it doesn't belong. He'd better watch out—it might get cut off.''

"He's doing his job.''

"Hassling hard-working citizens is his job? He needs to be rethinking his next election if that's how he defines his tasks.''

"It was a tip. He was checking it out.''

"Jody's had some problems, but he's straight now. I can vouch for him.'' Teo leaned back. "What happened at the widow's motel?''

Cole explained as briefly as possible, but before he'd even finished Teo was speaking. "Was anything taken?''

"No.''

"Then why in the hell would Jody Jackson just tear up this woman's room? What would he care?"

"Taylor thinks Cason might be behind it. Trying to run her off."

"Cason's been out of town for a month. He wouldn't have even known she was coming." Teo lifted one corner of his mouth. "If I were her, I'd be more concerned about upsetting the *fantasmas*. I hear they're pretty fierce at Diablo…hear they like it out there."

"Since when do you believe in ghosts?"

"I believe in everything, brother." He paused slightly. "You should, too."

Their eyes locked, and Cole felt a pulse of disquiet. He'd heard rumors that Teo dabbled in things he shouldn't. The locals came to him for spiritual help, believed he had powers Cole wasn't sure anyone held.

"Do you know where Jackson was that night?" Cole persisted.

"I don't keep track of the kids hour by hour."

"We had a dance that evening."

Both men turned and looked at Beryl, but she wasn't looking at them. She kept her back to them, her fingers tapping on the keyboard of the computer. It was the first time she'd spoken since Cole had entered the room. "Jody was here till after ten. I saw him." The tapping stopped and she turned around to stare at Cole. "It was our fall festival and he had a date. Jessica Gaskell."

"He could have done it before...or after."

She returned her attention to the keyboard without answering him. Teo looked at him with a smug expression. "Anything else, brother?"

Cole rose, feeling as if he'd been dismissed, and walked to the door. When Teo spoke again, Cole paused, one hand on the doorknob. "We found some minor shards near the border the other day and one or two utensil fragments. Looks pretty promising."

Teo had been searching for pottery for years, constantly had students from the University of Texas digging at a dozen different spots. They frequently dug near the river, where Mexico met Texas.

Tensing, Cole nodded. What did his brother know? What was he guessing? "That so?"

Teo looked into Cole's eyes as if he could read his mind from the inside out. "I think we might be getting close to finding something big."

"And what will you do once you find it?"

Teo didn't answer for a moment, then he grinned and held out his hands, the moment losing some of its immediate tension. "You'd better watch out, asking questions like that, Cole. You might give someone the mistaken feeling that you give a shit."

Cole glanced toward the corner where Beryl still typed. The clicking had slowed but it didn't stop. Cole turned back to Teo and put his hat on his head. "I'm not too worried about that happening, Teo. You'd be quick to correct them, I'm sure."

THE PHONE WAS RINGING when Taylor got back to her room. Juggling the box that contained the pot along with her coat and purse, she got to the receiver on the fifth ring. And wished she hadn't.

Richard's voice greeted her from the other end.

"I'd just about given up on you," he said, a cooler-than-usual tone in his voice. "I've been calling all morning. Where were you?"

She cradled the phone between her neck and shoulder and put her things on the bed. "I was out."

"Obviously. Doing what?"

She took a deep breath. "Making arrangements to come back to Houston."

There was a slight pause then he spoke, relief in his voice. "That's fantastic! When can I expect you, sweetheart?"

"Day after tomorrow."

"What time does your flight come in? I'll pick you up."

"I'd rather you didn't."

This time the silence lasted longer. "Why not? It's easier and I don't mind at all—"

She closed her eyes and rubbed the bridge of her nose. When she opened them again, she saw her reflection in the mirror across the room. There was a puffy darkness beneath her eyes and brackets on either side of her mouth. "Richard, I don't want to talk about it over the phone," she said gently. "Let me get there and we'll discuss it then."

He answered reluctantly. "Well, all right...if you

insist. I'll make reservations at Tony's. Meet me at the gallery and we'll go from there.''

She started to protest, then stopped. It would only upset him more if she said she wanted to have the discussion in private. ''I'll call you when I get in.''

''I'm looking forward to seeing you again. I've missed you.'' He stopped, obviously waiting for her to say the same.

''I—I've missed you, too,'' she said lamely. They said their goodbyes after that and slowly, she placed the receiver back in the cradle.

Was she doing the right thing? Was she merely infatuated with Cole? Had she made the right choice?

A knock sounded at her door, interrupting her thoughts. She opened it to find Cole on the doorstep.

''We need to talk,'' he said without preamble.

CHAPTER THIRTEEN

TAYLOR'S EYES WIDENED at his words. Then she stepped aside. "Come on in. I can make some coffee—"

"Not here." He tilted his head toward the street. "Come with me to the park. We'll talk there."

She studied him for just a second, then nodded. "I'll get my coat."

He waited for her on the sidewalk, not trusting himself to even step inside for a moment. Seeing that bed again, being in the room with her, was too much of a temptation, and the only way he could resist it was to avoid it.

She came outside wearing a new parka with a hood edged in white fur. She pulled the coat closer around her, then looked up at him as they started to walk down the sidewalk. "What's going on?"

"I talked to Teo," Cole said, hearing the grimness in his voice.

"What did he say? Anything new about the Jackson kid?"

"He said he could vouch for him, whatever that means. Then Beryl said Jackson had been at the fall festival on the day your room was trashed."

"All night?"

"Till ten. He still could have had time to do it."

Her shoulders slumped beneath the parka as they crossed the street, Cole taking her elbow. When they got to the other side, he didn't drop his hand. Wordlessly they made their way to the tiny park at the end of the block, Cole turning Taylor to look at him when they reached the shelter of the small gazebo in the center and sat on one of the benches lining its sides.

"But Teo mentioned his latest dig. Said they'd found some fairly important pieces."

Her expression reflected her confusion. "So? What has that got to do with anything?"

"Maybe nothing, but the question is—why did he bring it up?"

She arched her eyebrows.

"I think he may know there's pottery at Diablo...or at least suspect it."

"That's a pretty big leap, isn't it?"

"Not once you think about it." His fingers tightened around her arm. "He said he was hunting wolves the night we saw him, but there haven't been wolves at Diablo for fifty years."

"You think he was digging?"

"It's definitely a possibility."

"I don't understand."

Cole met Taylor's green eyes. "I don't, either, but something's going on, and I think he's involved."

Taylor nodded, and her gaze went over Cole's

shoulder to the mountains behind them. A disconnected expression came into her eyes, and he realized she wasn't listening as closely as he thought she would. "Taylor? What is it?"

She brought her gaze back to his face. "I spoke with Richard this morning. I—I'm going back to Houston, Cole."

A huge fist squeezed his heart. "Why did you decide to do this?"

"I thought about what you said last night."

He nodded, the giant grip moving up to his throat and closing there, preventing him from saying anything else.

"I have to tell Richard the truth," she said quietly. "I can't commit to him now. It wouldn't be fair—just as you said."

With unexpected suddenness, the invisible fingers released him, and Cole drew in a deep breath. "Not now? What's changed?" His heart stopped while he waited for her answer.

A quick puff of wind blew the white fur of her hood against her cheek. She reached up and pulled it away from her face. "Do you have to ask?"

In the silence of the park, a can rattled somewhere, the wind kicking it along.

Cole told himself not to, but he couldn't help it. He put a finger against her cheek and trailed it over the porcelain skin. "Then you're coming back?"

She nodded. "I have to."

He wanted to ask what she meant by that, but the

words wouldn't come out. And he knew why. If he wasn't the main reason she had to come back, he didn't want to know it. Not now. Not yet.

They rose by silent agreement and began the walk back to her motel. When they reached her door, Cole stopped. "I've got to go. I sent one group of clients out with another guide but I have to get ready for another group that's coming in next week."

A fleeting expression of disappointment came into Taylor's eyes before she could hide it. "Well, at least let me show you what I bought today," she said. "It's beautiful. Wait here and I'll get it."

She disappeared into the room, then came right back out. In the palm of her hand, she held a tiny pot he recognized immediately.

"I got it down at the gallery," she explained. "From Patricia Brown. Isn't it gorgeous?"

She handed it to him, and the memories that came with the smooth little pot almost overwhelmed him. Immediately he was in his mother's kitchen, smelling stew and listening to the wind rattle the windows. The barrage of emotions that accompanied the image weren't feelings he wanted to examine. He held the vase for a few seconds, then handed it back. "Nice," he said.

"The shard you found gave me a rough idea of what the pottery would look like, but I hadn't thought about the scale. It is perfect, isn't it?"

He nodded indifferently. "I thought you'd seen

this kind of thing before. Didn't Jack sell Indian pieces?''

She jerked her eyes to his, a puzzled expression shooting into her eyes before excitement replaced it. "You know, I think he did, now that you mention it. I thought it looked vaguely familiar but I figured that was because I'd seen the shard. It wasn't though.'' She shook her head in amazement. "I *did* see a piece similar to this in the shop. Several years ago. Obviously a replica. I'll have to ask Richard about it when I get back. He handles all the buying.''

Her words were innocuous, but like a wash of cold air, uneasiness came over Cole. "Where would he have gotten it?''

Taylor looked up at him, totally unaware of the turmoil he was experiencing. "Richard buys things like this all over the Southwest. He has a dealer in Taos who sells to him a lot. It might have been one of her pieces.''

Cole made the decision without even thinking. "What time are you leaving in the morning?'' he asked abruptly.

"At eight. My flight leaves Meader at ten-thirty. Why?''

"Would you like some company?''

Her fingers went to her throat. "T-to Houston? What about your clients?''

"I'll have time to prepare after I get back.'' The lie rolled easily off his tongue since it wasn't completely false. "Besides, I've got some business in Houston I've been putting off. There's a travel agent, a woman who handles a lot of executive types, who's been bugging me to set up some hunting trips. I need to see her. What do you say?"

"I think that'd be great."

"Then I'll drop off Lester and my barn keys at my neighbors and pick you up at seven-thirty."

He knew he shouldn't, but he was in so deep now it didn't even seem to matter anymore. Cole leaned down and kissed Taylor, hard and fast. When he pulled back, she wore a dazed expression. He turned and left.

TAYLOR DIDN'T UNDERSTAND, but she didn't care, either. All she knew was that Cole was coming with her to Houston, and suddenly she felt as if the weight of the world had been taken from her shoulders. She'd still have to face Richard alone, of course, but knowing Cole would be waiting for her afterward made the task somehow more bearable. His presence seemed to calm her—the dark, knowing eyes, a simple touch, his deep voice with its soft drawl...she hadn't realized he was affecting her that way until this very moment.

It was another thread connecting them, drawing them closer and closer.

Cole picked her up, and the trip went by fast. When their plane landed late the next day in Houston, Taylor wasn't prepared to be back. She stepped into the loud bustle of the busy terminal and almost felt assaulted. She hadn't seen this many people or heard this much noise in weeks. Before she'd left Houston, the antlike activity had just been part of life...now she saw it through new eyes. No one had time for anything but their own agenda. They rushed from one point to another, eyes down and determined, bleak expressions on their faces. She stood numbly beside the gate until Cole took her elbow in his hand and began to cut a path for them through the chaos to the line of taxis waiting outside the terminal.

His touch felt good against her arm, strong and supportive. She looked at him and her heart did a funny twist, bringing back thoughts of the kisses they'd shared, thoughts of the closeness growing between them and what it meant.

Oh, God...was she falling in love with Cole Reynolds?

Taylor barely noticed the drive. Twenty minutes later they were pulling up outside her condo complex close to the Galleria.

She hadn't been gone that long, but the house smelled musty and damp. She walked from room to room and opened the blinds, pulling back the draperies and turning on lights. When she'd made the circuit and returned to the living room, Cole was standing by one of the windows looking out into the central courtyard. It was a small space, even by condo standards, lined with brick pavers that led to a ten-foot wall decorated with a tiny fountain. A potted English ivy and two dead geraniums sat forlornly on either side of the dry basin.

"I'm not a very good gardener."

He turned around slowly and faced her. His hat was on the couch, but he hadn't taken off his coat, and his dark, intense presence seemed to fill up the room and suck out all the air. His eyes met hers and she felt something slick uncurl inside her, something alive with a mind of its own. She moved across the room and walked toward him.

His arms came out and pulled her the last few feet, but she didn't need the extra urging. Taylor lifted her own arms and locked them around his neck, his dark hair silky beneath her fingers as she tangled it in her hands. They came together in a collision of senses. She was overwhelmed by it all— his hands on her back, his lips at her throat, the scent of their desire rising between them.

She lost herself in the moment and gave in to the moment. Cole murmured and pulled her even closer, slipping one hand under her blouse to cup her breast. His thumb found her nipple and rubbed it, and she pressed herself closer into his touch. A moment later, his mouth captured hers, and Taylor actually felt herself go weak as his kiss sparked an even deeper flame of neediness inside her.

Then abruptly it was over.

Cole tore his mouth from hers and took two steps back. The instant, physical void she felt was incredible. It was so great, in fact, that she actually stumbled toward him, her hands out in supplication. He caught her and locked his fingers in hers, the heat between them almost fusing them together.

"I can't do this." His eyes were hot and glowing. "I can't keep kissing you without it leading to more."

"Then why stop?" She moved closer, her eyes searching his, her body heavy with desire. "We're adults, Cole. We can make our own choices—"

"And I'm choosing to stop," he said harshly. "Until you talk to Richard, that's what has to happen."

"But I'm going to tell him tonight."

"Fine. Tell him tonight. And after you've done that, then we can make our choices. But not before."

"Why are you doing this?" she whispered. "Don't you want me?"

He closed his eyes for just a second, then pulled himself together with obvious difficulty. "I want you more than I've ever wanted a woman. I can *taste* it I want you so much—can taste *you*. But I'll be damned if I make love to you before you've talked to Richard. And I mean that literally." He dropped her hands, then turned and picked up his hat. Striding toward the door, he stopped when his boots hit the marble entry and swiveled to look at her. "What's the address of the gallery?"

She told him, her voice wooden, her body numb, desire still pounding through it.

"I'll stop by at nine. We can come back here together when it's over."

She nodded.

"This is the best way, Taylor." His voice pulled her eyes up, and when their gazes locked something sparked between them. It rippled over her body, leaving a trail of fire behind it. She knew the tingling wouldn't stop until she was in his arms again. "I'll see you tonight."

"Tonight..." she said. But the door had already closed and she was speaking to an empty room.

TAYLOR WANDERED FROM room to room after Cole left, touching this or that, picking up a pillow and moving it, rearranging a shelf of books. It was aimless, stupid activity—just something to keep her hands busy while her mind whirled round and round. It had been years since she'd felt this kind of sexual desire, she thought numbly. It was remarkable.

Taking a deep breath and putting everything else from her mind, she finally picked up the phone to call Richard, but he wasn't in. The relief she felt was overwhelming. She left a message with Martha telling him not to make reservations for dinner and that she'd see him at the gallery at eight.

She resumed her roaming after the call, Cole on her mind, and by the time she realized she needed to dress for the meeting, she was running late. She showered in record time then put on a minimal amount of makeup, a little blush and some mascara, a dash of lipstick and nothing more. Twisting her hair up on her head, she stuck a long barrette into it and prayed it would stay. The hardest decision was what to wear. She stared at the rows of dresses and suddenly marveled at all the clothes. Why on earth did she have so many? What did she need them all for? Had she really gone out that much? During the time she'd been in High Mountain, she'd worn nothing but jeans and sweaters and had gotten by just fine. Did a woman really need this many clothes?

She ended up pulling out a black silk skirt and a matching blouse. The fabric felt cold on her skin then quickly warmed, and she realized she'd never noticed that before. She rubbed her fingers up and down her arm and remembered Cole's hot touch. Had he somehow made her more aware of everything? In the bathroom mirror, she watched as her fingers went to her mouth and pressed against her lips, mimicking the feel of the kiss they'd shared. What had he done to her?

What *would* he do to her?

Turning around and fleeing the wild-eyed woman in the mirror, Taylor grabbed her purse and her car keys. Within minutes she was on Richmond Avenue, heading east. The traffic was worse than she remembered but that was fine. It took her thoughts off herself. When she pulled up in front of the gallery, fifteen minutes later, she didn't even remember the drive.

Richard's black Lexus was under the porte

cochere, and off to the left, where the offices were, there were lights on inside. The gallery itself—the center section of the building—was mostly dark. Looking right and left, Taylor made her way to the middle where a huge set of custom-designed doors, heavy mahogany and beveled glass, towered. She pulled out her key ring and started to put one into the lock when she realized the doors were open. Pushing them aside, she walked into the gallery, her footsteps echoing on the polished tile entry.

"Richard? Are you here?"

No one answered and Taylor felt a quiver of unease. She'd never liked the gallery at night. In the darkness, the African masks on the walls seemed to move, catching her peripheral vision yet standing still when she faced them head-on. The totem pole Richard had bought last year in Sitka lurked even taller in the shadows, and she could have sworn she heard the grass skirt of the Zulu tribal king rustle in one corner. She swallowed and moved toward the office. "Richard?"

Nothing but silence answered her, and Taylor had to convince herself to keep going because what she really wanted was to turn around and run the other way. For some strange reason she thought of the ranch and the rumors of haunting that refused to go away.

She forced herself forward and made her way down the darkened corridor toward Richard's office. Light spilled out into the hallway from the interior so he had to be there somewhere, she figured. Maybe he'd stepped into the bathroom or the tiny kitchenette they had behind the reception area and hadn't heard her call out.

Her steps slowed as she reached the doorway, then stopped completely as she came even with the opening and the circular wooden desk where Martha usually sat. The light was coming from her and Richard's office, she realized, and she called out one more time. "Richard? Are you here?"

She sensed the movement behind her a second too late. The hand fell on her shoulder and she screamed.

COLE MISSED THE OLD police station. The dirty, much-abused building down on Riesner had had character. The newly renovated skyscraper towering over downtown looked too much like all the other buildings around it. Anonymous and generic. It could have housed insurance agents as easily as it housed cops.

Walking into the bustling lobby, Cole looked around and quickly spotted Danny Booker. His friend was six feet, four inches tall and even here, with dozens of other Texas-sized cops milling around, he managed to stand out. His height had something to do with that fact, but it might have been the way he looked, too. A thousand-dollar suit did that for a man. To move in the circles he did, it was necessary, though, and the department agreed with him. He was the only cop on the force with a clothes allowance.

Danny broke away from the men he'd been talking to and strode toward Cole with his hand outstretched and a smile on his face. "Cole—damn, it's good to see you."

The two men shook hands then grinned at each other and hugged. They went back a long way, further than Cole wanted to remember, even past his Navy Special Ops days.

"I couldn't believe it when you called," Danny said. "What the hell are you doing in the big city?"

"I'll explain in a minute, but first...you're still in the art fraud division, aren't you?"

"Are you kidding? I'll be there till I die. No one else around here gives a damn about it but me. They'd rather chase down killers and dopers." He fingered his lapels. "Now I ask you...why would I want to give up threads like these to chase crooks like that?"

Cole grinned at the act, but he knew how seriously Danny took his job and why. He'd come from an incredibly wealthy Texas family and his mother had been kidnapped when she was twenty-five in exchange for a painting. The kidnappers had never been found, but his mother had. In a shallow grave near Galveston.

Cole nodded. "Then let's go upstairs and I'll explain."

A few minutes later, they were sitting by Danny's desk, two cups of sludgelike coffee beside them.

"I've got this friend," Cole started.

"A woman, of course."

He looked at Danny above the rim of his mug. "Yes, a woman... And she's—"

"Got a problem?"

"Are you gonna let me explain?"

Danny held up his hands and grinned. "Just trying to cut to the chase."

"I can do that myself, thanks." But could he? Since he'd left Taylor's condo, Cole had thought of nothing but her and tonight. He'd wanted her for so long...

"As you were saying?"

He focused once more, ignoring Danny's expression. "I want to know what you know about a guy named Richard Williams. He's an art—"

"Dealer here in Houston. Very upper crust." Danny sipped his coffee then grimaced and put the cup down. "He's part owner in a gallery over off Westheimer called Matthews/Williams. His partner was killed two or three years ago out in..." His words slowly died.

"Out in High Mountain," Cole finished. "And his widow is a friend of mine. It's a long story and all I have is a hunch. I just want to see if the guy is on the up and up."

"As far as I know, he's never done anything illegal..."

"But?"

Danny shrugged. "There are always rumors about these guys, even when there's no truth to them. The competition is fierce so if one of 'em gets ticked off, he's just as likely to call up here and report something as he is to call the IRS. They like to think they're getting each other in trouble. Is there a connection to the partner's death?"

"Not that I know about. I just found myself wondering about the stuff he sold. Taylor—my friend—told me she thought Williams might have sold some Jumano pottery a few years ago, and that got me interested. Can't say exactly why."

"Old or new?"

Cole shrugged. "She didn't know."

"Old would be rare. Rare and expensive. It'd have to be certified, too, by the Indian Council. Now if it wasn't certified…"

Cole leaned forward. "There'd be a problem, right?"

"Oh, yeah. A big problem. All kinds of federal regs on that."

"But who would buy illegal pottery without certification?"

Danny shook his head and leaned back. "You'd be amazed—sometimes I think these dealers like it more if it's hot. Adds to the cachet, somehow. Indiana Jones and all that bullshit…"

"But they can't show it to anyone, can they?"

"Sure they can—to all their other buddies who

buy illegal art. There's a real underground market out there, Cole, and as I said, it's as cutthroat as hell. But hey—that keep's me working, right?''

Cole nodded slowly.

Danny turned to a file drawer on his left. Rummaging around in the mess, he pulled out a battered file, flipped through it, then selected a black-and-white photo. He tossed it across the desk. ''An HPD undercover photographer took that last year at a charity function for me. That's Williams in the right-hand corner of the photo, his girlfriend's on the left. I was investigating the woman to his right. There had been some talk the woman and Williams were into something. She was bringing in icons from Russia and you wouldn't believe where she was stashing them—that's another story, though. Anyway, Williams checked out okay when we were looking into this situation. Hell, you can tell by looking at the guy he'd be straight. He's too damned boring to be anything else. On the other hand, his name does keep cropping up from time to time.''

Cole picked up the photo and stared at the grainy image, his gaze skipping over the woman he didn't know and going straight to Richard Williams. He was a distinguished-looking man. Tall and nicely tanned with the physique of someone much younger, he had silver hair and wore a suit even more expensive than Danny's, highlighting his wide shoulders and deep chest. His bearing was regal yet casual, as if he'd had money for so long he'd forgotten what it took to get it.

And standing beside him was Taylor.

She wore a long, elegant gown, the material dark and sensual as it clung to her every curve, the slit up one side open just enough for the camera to catch a hint of the smooth legs underneath. There were diamonds at her throat and wrist, and a crystal flute of champagne in her fingers. Even her hair looked different. The golden strands had been twisted and tucked against her head to fashion a smooth coil totally unlike the haphazard knot he was accustomed to seeing. She looked completely foreign to the woman he knew in jeans and oversized sweaters. A sinking feeling started in his gut and traveled downward, accompanied by an insistent voice. *This,* the voice said, is the real Taylor Matthews, so what in the hell do you think you're doing?

He realized too late Danny was staring at him.

"Boy…you got it baaad, don't you?" The detective shook his head, his expression suddenly sober. "I think I better get you down to the Crystal Pistol and get you exorcised. Bubba's got a new dancer down there by the name of Heather. She's a redhead—a *real* redhead—and she can do things with that pole you wouldn't believe—"

Cole stood abruptly. "Thanks for the help." His fingers crushed the brim of his hat.

"Well, sure," Danny said, coming to his feet, his eyes holding genuine concern now. "Anytime, you know that. I wouldn't mind nailing the bastard if he is into anything illegal. Meantime, I hope I helped."

Cole met his friend's look. "You've helped a lot, old friend." He put on his hat. "Made me see what a damned fool I've really been. I'll be in touch."

CHAPTER FOURTEEN

TAYLOR SPUN AROUND, her heart crashing against her ribs, her breath stopping inside her chest. For a moment she stood immobile, then her scream choked before it could escape, her fright giving way to anger.

"Oh, my God, Richard! You scared the daylights out of me! What in the hell—"

"Taylor, Taylor…" Richard held her forearms, steadying her. "Who did you expect, sweetheart? You were calling for me. I thought—"

"You should have answered," she said with exasperation, pulling her arms away from him and straightening her skirt. "I didn't expect you to just grab me like that."

"I didn't grab you." His voice was mild and vaguely puzzled. "I assumed you heard me walk up. I didn't mean to scare you, darling. I'm sorry… Why didn't you ring the bell?"

"The front door was unlocked."

He looked back toward the hall. "Oh, I didn't know. I'll go lock it, then we can leave." He started walking toward the door. "Martha gave me a message, but she obviously got it wrong. She said you didn't want to go to dinner—'' He stopped when he realized she wasn't following. "Taylor?"

"I don't want to go to dinner, Richard. I'd really prefer to just stay here and talk, if you don't mind."

His face was in the shadows so she couldn't read his expression, but his body seemed to tense. "I made reservations, sweetheart. I'd hate to cancel them."

She took two steps toward him, the darkness surrounding them. "I know. But this is important."

"All right." His voice was as understanding as always, but a hint of exasperation seeped out. "Let's go into the chapel, then. We won't be disturbed if the phone rings."

She followed him to the exhibition room that made up the right wing of the building. They'd called it the chapel ever since they'd opened the gallery—the first showing they'd held there had been a group of religious triptychs done by an Azerbaijani refugee in the late eighties. The room *seemed* chapel-like as well. With a high ceiling and timbered beams that met in the middle, arched windows lining the sides, each highlighted by a down light, it was always quiet and peaceful. Jack had designed every aspect of the room, even down to the tapestry chairs scattered around the perimeter, one of which Richard now pulled out for Taylor in a gesture of courtesy.

He sat down beside her, then leaned over and took

one of her hands. "All right," he said quietly. "I'm
all yours. You talk, I'll listen."

His words sent her into the past. Countless times,
after Jack's death, Richard had found her in this very
spot, tears pouring from her eyes, grief welling out
of her from a source that seemed to have no end.
He'd held her hands, just like this, and listened,
never judging, never complaining, never doing anything more than offering his shoulder. She wondered
briefly if he'd brought her here now because of that
or if he'd chosen the spot by accident. Either way
it didn't really matter. She'd made up her mind and
nothing was going to change it now.

Taking a deep breath, she brought her eyes to his.
"Richard—this is very, very hard for me to say."
She stopped and gently pulled her hands from his
grasp. "Since Jack's death you've been a real rock
for me. Always there, always helping. You'll never
know what your support and understanding have
done for me."

"I'm glad you feel that way. Helping you is all
I've ever wanted to do."

She smiled gently. "And I'll always be grateful.
But the truth is, feeling grateful isn't enough, not for
the kind of relationship you want or deserve. I
thought it was—thought that getting engaged was a
good thing to do—but it isn't, and I can't go on
letting you think it's going to happen." She stopped
and drew a deep breath. "I'm sorry, Richard, but I

can't commit to you. It wouldn't be fair.'' She handed him the velvet box with the ring in it.

Looking at the box in his hand, he let her words die out in the silence of the room, then he spoke, sadness filling his voice. ''I was afraid that was what you were going to say.''

''I feel terrible, and I know this isn't the way to repay you for all you did, but if we married I think we'd both be making a terrible mistake.'' She dropped her voice. ''I—I don't love you as a wife should love a husband.''

''I could make you love me that way. In time.''

She shook her head. ''I don't think so. Love doesn't work like that. It either happens…or it doesn't.''

He sighed and looked out the window. When he turned back to face her, his eyes gleamed in the dim light. ''I knew when you went out to the ranch there would be trouble. That's why I tried so desperately to keep you here.''

''But I had to go—''

''Not really,'' he said gently. ''You could have left everything alone, Taylor, and we would have been fine. Just fine.''

''Neither of us would have been happy if we'd married.''

''I disagree entirely. We might not have had what you and Jack had, but our marriage would have been good. I know it.''

''But sooner or later…'' She let her voice fade

away. "This is for the best, and someday you'll agree with me, I'm sure."

He shook his head. "I don't see how, but maybe you're right. Things always work out as they're supposed to, don't they?" He stood, a distinguished, solitary figure. Standing in front of the nearest window, he put his hands behind his back as he stared out into the night. He stayed there for a few minutes, still as a statue, then he turned and spoke. "Is there another man?"

Shocked by the abrupt and unexpected question, Taylor suddenly felt an electrical kind of tension. It hovered in the air between them. Like a live wire. She rose from her chair, her throat tight. "Richard, I—I don't think I made myself very clear. I'm not breaking off with you because there's someone else. I—I just think it's the right thing to do. We came together when I was really needy and now—"

"And now you're stronger…and you don't need me anymore…but you still didn't answer my question."

"I am stronger," she said quietly, her heart breaking at the tone in his voice. "And if there was someone else in my life he wouldn't be the reason for this. I just don't think we have enough between us to make a real relationship." Walking toward him, she stopped. "I should never have taken the ring, Richard. I…I knew then I wasn't ready and frankly I know now you were right when you said I was using my need for closure as an excuse to put you off.''

His expression tightened, but he nodded without saying a word. Taylor stood awkwardly beside him. Finally she spoke. "I'll come back in the morning and we can discuss the business situation.''

He stared down at the box still in his hand, then he spoke very slowly, his voice holding a hint of anger for the first time. "There is nothing to discuss about the 'business' situation, as you put it, Taylor. I own half of Matthews/Williams. That is not going to change.''

She looked at him in surprise. "But Richard, we can't work together. Not now.''

"Why not?''

"Well, it'd be too awkward, too...messy.''

"Too messy...'' She watched uneasily as he opened the box and lifted the diamond out of its soft bed to hold it up to the light. His eyes settled on the flashing stone, and her gaze did the same, but a moment later, their gaze collided over the ring.

In the dim light of the room, his eyes seemed to glitter as sharply as the diamond. She shivered, then told herself she was being silly. This was Richard—dear, safe Richard.

He spoke softly, quietly. "You've made a mistake, Taylor, darling.'' Each word came out distinctly with a slight pause between every one. "A very big mistake.''

"I think that's for the lady to say, isn't it?''

At the sound of Cole's voice, Taylor turned. He was standing directly behind her, his tall, dark form filling the doorway, the open flaps of his leather duster flaring beside his legs. The top of his hat almost brushed the header on the door. He looked at her and raised one eyebrow, and she felt a flood of relief so intense it threatened to pull her under. Only then did she realize how scared she'd been.

She slowly looked at Richard. He was staring at Cole with a measured glance, but he didn't say a word. Finally his eyes moved to Taylor. Something dark and unsettling lurked in his stare, something she'd never seen before. She didn't know what it was, but she didn't want to know, either.

She turned around and without even a glance back, she walked toward Cole.

TAYLOR HANDED COLE the car keys when they got outside the gallery. He took them silently, then opened the car door for her. Thirty minutes later they were at the condo, without a single word passing between them.

Taylor walked inside, ahead of him, and stopped by the kitchen sink. Looking out the window, she spoke quietly. "Can I fix you something to drink?"

"Why don't you go sit down and relax? Let me do the fixing."

Her fingers gripped the edge of the ceramic tile and she spoke as though he hadn't said anything. "There's all kinds of liquor in the bar over there, and I think I left some beer in the refrigerator. It might be old, though. If you'd prefer wine instead—"

She broke off when he came up behind her and put his hands on her shoulders. In the window above the sink, she met his eyes in the reflection. They stared at each other for a moment, then Cole eased her around, the black silk of her blouse smooth and sensual beneath his fingers. She wore a pinched expression, as if she were trying hard not to cry.

"It's over now. The hard part is past."

She nodded slowly.

"He wasn't a bastard about it, was he?"

She hesitated for only a second, then spoke. "N-no. Richard isn't that kind of man."

Cole tightened his fingers. "Good."

"But he said I was making a mistake."

"Of course he did. He's losing you. Any man in his right mind would see that as a mistake." Cole took her chin between his thumb and finger and tilted it up. "But it isn't. And you know that, don't you?"

She nodded slowly.

"And you know why, don't you?"

She nodded again.

Their lips came together slowly, almost tentatively. Leaning back against the counter, Taylor hesitated slightly, then she moved closer and wrapped her arms around his neck. Cole brought her body toward his, hip to hip, chest to chest. Every point of contact was a lit fire.

After a moment, she pulled back and looked up at him. "What's happening between us?"

"Nothing you don't want to happen."

She stared at him a moment longer, then she stepped back, leaving an awful void in his arms and in his heart. And in that instant, he remembered the photo he'd seen in Danny's office. Of the sophisticated Taylor, of the elegant Taylor, of the Taylor who wouldn't give a man like him a second look. His breath caught painfully in his chest as he told himself he was the biggest fool in the world.

Then she took his hand and led him out of the room. They went up the stairs and didn't stop until they were standing beside her bed.

TAYLOR BEGAN TO slowly unbutton Cole's shirt. When the starched white cotton fell open, she closed her eyes and slid her fingers inside, her palms flattening against his chest, the muscles corded and hard beneath her touch. She breathed deeply, pulling in his scent and making it a part of her. Then she laid her head against his chest.

His gentle hands cradled her head and smoothed her hair. She reveled in the deliberate, sensual stroking, and when she looked up at him, her heart started a deep, heavy thudding that echoed along every line of her body.

He bent down and kissed her, then he murmured

something in the back of his throat. Not even understanding what he'd said, she answered with a groan of her own as Cole's fingers found the buttons of her silk blouse and unfastened them. He parted the fabric and brought her closer to him, her breasts pressing against his bare chest, the warmth of their mutual desire building between them.

Moments later, she shed the rest of her clothing and in an instant she was standing before him in the filtered light from the hallway. He moved back, just a step, and let his gaze go slowly down her body. A hot ripple of need followed in the wake of his stare, and Taylor lifted her hands to her throat, her fingers spreading out over her chest then cupping her breasts. He continued to look steadily at her, then he reached out slowly and put his hands over hers.

"You're beautiful," he said in a low, thick voice. "Too beautiful."

They stood there together, their hands entwined, their eyes meeting, then Taylor moved closer and peeled his shirt off his shoulders. Everything else came off as well, and there was nothing she could do but look, too.

His body was lean and hard, the kind of hard that came from honest work and hours of labor. Wide shoulders, muscular chest, hips that were slim and tight. She reached out and ran her hands over him. The body beneath her fingers was smooth, and the ache inside built even more.

He pulled her toward him, then unexpectedly lifted her, cupping her buttocks with his hands and bringing her closer to him with an ease that made it obvious her weight was no strain. Dipping his head, he began to kiss her breasts, first one and then the other, his tongue leaving a hot wetness in its wake, a trail of burning desire. She arched her back and his mouth went to her neck, gentle kisses that teased her and made her want him even more, although she wouldn't have thought that possible.

All at once he turned and placed her on the bed. Her hips barely touched the edge as he knelt beside her and began to kiss the inside of her thighs. He worked his way slowly upward, and every place his mouth touched, Taylor felt a pinprick of heat. Finally all the points were connected and the desires he'd been building inside her reached an explosive level. She cried out, helpless in his hands as he continued, his mouth going to her belly, her breasts, her throat. Only when he captured her mouth in a kiss did her groans turn to silence.

He entered her a second later.

Taylor wrapped her legs around him and the rhythm built between them. At that moment, that very moment, she realized what she'd never understood before. The brush with death that she and Cole had shared so long ago had connected them, had fused them together with pain and grief and impossibly deep emotions. Together, they'd built a relationship unlike anything she'd had with anyone else.

And it scared her to death.

She tightened her arms around his neck and gazed into the black, endless depths of his eyes. As if he understood the realization she'd just come to, he nodded, then he bent his head and placed his mouth on hers. A few seconds later, their muffled cries came at the very same time.

COLE WOKE UP at 3 a.m. For one heartstopping second, he had no idea where he was, then slowly reality returned and he heard Taylor's deep, easy breathing beside him. He turned his head and looked at her. In the darkness, her profile was sharp and well-defined, her nose straight and narrow, her chin pointed and determined. Knowing he shouldn't but unable to resist, he reached out and traced a finger down the softer line of her cheek. She murmured in her sleep and moved closer to him.

He opened his arms and pulled her into the circle of his embrace.

CHAPTER FIFTEEN

COLE WAS GONE when she woke up.

Sitting up in the bed, the morning sun coming through the shutters on the nearby windows, Taylor knew immediately that Cole wasn't in the house. More than silence filled the room—there was a void, an empty kind of solitude, that told her she was the only one around. She glanced to the table where she always put her keys. They were gone. He'd probably run down to the bakery on the corner for doughnuts or bread. There was nothing in the house to eat.

She rolled to one edge of the bed and climbed out, reaching for the robe she normally left on the chair, then remembered why it wasn't there. Walking naked to the closet, she pulled out the first thing her hand found—an old T-shirt—and slipped it on. Downstairs she filled the German coffeemaker with coffee from the freezer, then stared out the kitchen window with her mug in her hand and waited. When she took her first sip, she frowned. It didn't taste nearly as good as the black brew from Cole's enamel pot. And the view out the window wasn't nearly as nice, either. From a place she'd kept hidden for a very long time, Taylor felt a longing well up, a longing for big spaces and faraway views and God-made silences that caused your heart to catch from the wonder of it all.

She didn't know what to make of the yearning, just as she didn't know what to think about last night. Richard had appeared to take her rejection fairly well, but something about their conversation had scared her. She told herself she was being silly. After the hours she'd spent in bed with Cole last night, she couldn't be sure about anything. Thinking of either man right now was more than she could handle.

The groan of the garage door caught her attention and she set her coffee mug down on the kitchen counter and headed for the back door. Cole was pulling her car into the garage when she opened it. He climbed out with a bag of doughnuts in one hand and a sack of groceries in the other. Through the plastic, she could see milk and eggs, apples and pears, a huge bunch of grapes…and a single red rose.

"Good mornin'." His slow West Texas drawl sent shivers up and down her spine as he crossed the garage and came into the kitchen. "I didn't expect to see you up when I got back. You were out of it when I left."

She imagined him watching her while she slept. The intimacy of the vision unfurled a red warning flag within her. What was she getting herself into?

He put the groceries down on the counter, then

pulled the rose from the bag. Holding the thick, green stem, he drew the bloodred petals over one side of her face, and then down the other. She sucked in a breath as he tracked the flower down her neck to the open V of her T-shirt where it finally rested on the swell of one breast. He kept the petals there for a second, cold and soft, then he handed the flower to her.

"Thank you," she said thickly.

"You're very welcome."

He leaned over to kiss her, but Taylor began to fuss with the coffee paraphernalia, a suffocating band of awkwardness suddenly cutting off her air. Behind her, there was a moment's silence, then she heard Cole begin to unload the groceries. When she turned around, with a full cup of coffee ready for him, she saw that he'd put the doughnuts on a plate and was waiting for her. She sat down beside him, his presence filling up the tiny breakfast room. Her thoughts swirled around in confusion.

He sipped from his coffee then put the mug down carefully. "I talked to a friend of mine last night," he said quietly. "He works at HPD."

Obviously sensing her mental chaos, he wanted to make the morning as painless as possible. An impersonal topic of conversation was much easier than discussing what had happened between them. She drew a breath of relief. "A policeman?"

"A detective. He's in the art fraud division."

Cole looked up and met her eyes. "Did you know they investigated Richard a few years ago?"

Taylor's mouth actually dropped open. "What?"

"I don't know all the details, but apparently he was involved with someone who was selling smuggled goods from Russia."

"Are you sure about this?"

"My friend is reliable."

In shock, Taylor stared across the table at Cole. "I never heard anything about it."

"I'm sure you wouldn't. It's not something Richard would want to share, is it?" He tapped a rhythm on the tabletop with one finger, then looked up at her. "How well do you actually know this guy, Taylor?"

Frowning, she sipped her coffee. "He was Jack's partner for years, and Jack was a pretty good judge of character. I don't think he would have picked a crook to go into business with…"

"I'm sure he wouldn't have, and maybe Richard's completely legit. But he *was* investigated. And it makes me wonder if there's a connection here we're missing."

"What kind of connection?"

"I don't know exactly—I guess I'm just thinking out loud." His lifted his eyes to her face. "But if Williams was somehow selling authentic Jumano pottery, the pieces could only come from the High Mountain area, even if they went through another dealer first."

"And that's why he didn't want me going out there?"

"It's a possibility. Maybe he was afraid you'd find out he was selling something he shouldn't have been."

"If they were authentic and not certified…"

"Or…if they were stolen…"

She leaned back in her chair, her stomach churning. "God, do you think that's possible? Could I have been around him this much and never really known him?"

"Sometimes we're fooled." Cole turned and looked out the window, his profile sharp and unforgiving. "I loved a woman once, loved her like you loved Jack. But I wanted to leave High Mountain. I was young and thought if I could get out of there for a while, it'd solve all my problems. I joined the Navy and told her we'd get married in a year, when I came back. She promised to wait for me."

Taylor turned still. "And?"

"And…she didn't wait. The letters stopped coming, and when I couldn't find her, I called my mother and she told me the truth. My girlfriend not only didn't wait, she married someone else." His voice was measured and calm, and he told the story as if he were recounting something that had happened to someone else, not himself. But his eyes gave him away. Time had eased the hurt, but it was still there. "She married my brother."

Taylor's breath caught and for a moment she

couldn't say anything. Finally she found her voice.
"Beryl? Beryl was your fiancée?"

"Yes."

He drained his coffee cup, rose from the table and
went to the sink. She stared at his stiff, straight back,
confused and unable to think of anything to say.

"Do you see what I'm telling you, Taylor? We
all make mistakes." He turned to face her. "I was
a poor judge of character. I thought the person I saw
was really the person who was there. I wasn't smart
enough—or old enough—to understand that even
the best of us can be fooled. Betrayal comes in a lot
of different ways."

"But something must have happened. Did you
talk to her—ask her what—"

"I don't mean Beryl, Taylor." His voice was soft,
forgiving. "She was a pawn in the whole thing,
someone handy who could be used to prove a point.
I'm talking about my brother. He's a bastard with
no morals and he taught me a hard lesson I've never
forgotten. You can never really know another person, not completely. You may think you do, but you
don't, not really. And it's a mistake to believe anything else."

THE TRIP BACK to High Mountain was quiet, but full
of tension. After revealing what he had, Cole with-
drew behind an emotional wall that Taylor knew she
wouldn't be able to penetrate. After a while, she
wasn't sure she wanted to. She needed time herself,

time to think about the past twenty-four hours and everything that had happened.

There was only one problem, though. She could have all the time in the world, and she had the feeling she still wouldn't know what to do. All she really wanted was to get back to High Mountain and that scared her as much as anything. The longing she felt to breathe the clean air and to let her eyes drink in the lonely landscape was definitely something she hadn't counted on. Any more than she had counted on falling in love with Cole Reynolds.

She turned and looked at him.

In the stark light pouring through the airplane window, his features were sharp and angular, and all she could do was close her eyes against the sudden pain—and sudden truth—she was finally being forced to accept, although she'd known long before they'd made love. She loved Cole and loved him far too much.

How in the world had she let this happen?

Falling in love meant that you were vulnerable, that you could be hurt. That you might lose the person and the blackness would come and swallow you up again.

She hadn't wanted to love anyone again as she'd loved Jack. That's why she'd been lulled into something with Richard. She'd wanted a safe, almost arm's length, relationship. If she didn't fall in love too deeply, then she'd survive if it didn't work out.

So what had she done instead? She'd gone and

fallen in love with Cole. And the connection they shared was definitely *not* an arm's length one…and there wasn't a thing she could do about it now. It was too late. Her heart was already involved.

It was late by the time they saw the lights of the town twinkling in the distance. The weather had gotten colder, the air crisp and sharp, the smell of fires lingering to add another layer. Cole pulled his pickup truck into a parking spot at the motel and turned to look at her.

"So what are your plans now? Are you going back to Shipley or—"

She interrupted his question by raising her hand and stopping him. He fell instantly silent, his dark eyes on hers. "Cole, about last night… I—I hope you won't get mad but—"

"But what?"

She shook her head. "I think it might be best if we don't repeat what happened." She hesitated. "I hope you understand."

His dark eyes glittered. "Why? Why this change of heart?"

How could she explain? How could she make him understand how much it terrified her that she had fallen in love with him. Terrified her because it meant her life would be empty without him, and that she couldn't even risk the possibility. How could she explain?

She couldn't. So she lied and said the first thing that came into her mind.

KAY DAVID   239

"Because there's nowhere for it to go," she answered. "When this is over, you'll return to your life in High Mountain, and I'll...I'll end up in Houston."

"And what if you didn't go back?" he asked quietly.

"I—I have to," she said, not looking at him. "My life is in Houston. My friends, my home...my work."

A cold silence built in the cab of the truck, and the longer it took for Cole to answer, the chillier it became. Finally he spoke, his voice weary with acceptance. "I understand, Taylor. I knew this was going to happen anyway." She turned and looked at him and he reached out to draw his finger down her cheek. "You're right. It won't work. Your world is different than mine. I really do understand."

Her eyes filled with tears. "No, you don't," she whispered, "but that's all right." She leaned over and kissed him. Then she opened the door of the truck and fled.

COLE THOUGHT LONG and hard over the next two days, mainly about Taylor.

The time they'd shared had been incredible and he knew as long as he lived, he'd never forget it. Since the moment he'd slipped from her sheets, he'd wanted to pull her back into his arms and kiss her, then take off all her clothes and repeat everything they'd done, plus add a few more activities he had no trouble thinking up. Her smooth, white skin, her perfect breasts, the way her back dipped just above her buttocks—the images tormented him and they would for a very long time. Because they were all he would ever have for the rest of his life. He'd known that since the moment he'd met her and that fact had only been reinforced when he'd seen the photo of her and Richard Williams. Ignoring the truth, Cole had let his emotions take over, and he'd made love to her, knowing it couldn't happen again, setting himself up for the fall.

He hadn't been surprised by her words in the truck. In fact, he'd expected them, and if she hadn't said them to him, he had a suspicion he would have said them to her.

That didn't make it any easier, though.

The following morning when he drove into town to pick up his next group of hunters, he went down Oak Street instead of Main, to avoid her motel. Leaving Lester in the truck, Cole slipped into the diner from the back. He surveyed the room quickly and seeing no sign of Taylor, took a rear booth and ordered his breakfast. Before his meal arrived, he looked up from the local paper to see J. C. Shipley standing beside his table.

"Mind if I join you?"

Hiding his surprise, Cole hesitated, but Shipley was already sliding his girth into the space between the table and the plastic red bench. He put his sweat-stained hat on the seat beside him and met Cole's eyes.

"I wanna talk to you about Miz Matthews," Shipley said.

Cole's heart thudded, and he half rose from the table. "What's wrong? Is she okay—"

"She's fine, she's fine…far as I know. Sit back down." Shipley leaned closer and put his elbows on the table. "This is about what happened before. You know, her tires, her motel room…even her brakes, I guess."

Shipley's tone was odd, out of sync with his usual, blustery self-confidence.

Cole nodded slowly. "Go on."

"I know who did it. All of it." He looked down at the table, then up at Cole. "I knew about it before it even happened."

"What the hell are you saying, J.C.?"

The uniformed man leaned even closer. "I got a call from Houston a while back. I didn't know who it was—shit, I still don't know who it was—but they said if I looked the other way while a few things happened here in town, I'd have plenty of money in my campaign chest next November."

Cole's voice was tight when he spoke. "You sure it was from Houston?"

"It was a 713 area code. That's Houston all right."

Cole immediately thought of a tall, well-built older man. Richard Williams.

Shipley licked his lips nervously and spoke again. "To prove their intentions, the guy said they'd send down an early donation. And they did." He swallowed hard. "I took out fifty dollars then put the rest in a drawer and went over to the motel. I paid the clerk to put her in a room with no one on either side and to make himself scarce that night it happened. Then her room was trashed."

A rush of anger so intense it took his breath came over Cole. He felt his jaw tighten and he tensed the rest of his body, forcing himself into stillness.

"Who did it?"

"I don't know exactly."

"Make a guess."

"I'd have to point the finger at Jody Jackson—just like I told her later."

"He make the phone calls and slice her tires, too?"

"I don't know, but I'd say that's a fair guess. The guy on the phone said he just wanted to scare her, so he probably started out easy with the calls and all."

Cole's mouth curled up in disgust. "How could you do this, J.C.? I thought you were a better man."

For a moment, Shipley looked sheepish, then he shrugged. "Life's different out here, Cole, and you know it. We play by another set of rules. I figured as long as nobody got hurt, it wouldn't matter."

"As long as nobody…" Cole shook his head in amazement. "She could have been killed when the brakes went out. And that shot out at the ranch was damned close!''

''I know,'' the older man said bleakly. ''And I'm not prepared to be a part of no murder scheme. I didn't think it'd go that far. That's why I'm telling you this. I got another call last night, and I think something else is gonna happen, but I don't know what. I told the son of a bitch to forget about it—I was sending back his dirty money, but he just laughed. Said he could blackmail me now for taking a bribe. Said I damn well better help him.''

The big man's jaw twitched, then tightened. ''I don't have to take that kinda shit from nobody. Problem is I can't go to Miz Matthews now. She wouldn't listen to me if I did. She thinks I'm an idiot who can't do my job and besides that, I insinuated some pretty nasty stuff. I thought if I made her mad enough, she'd just leave, but it didn't work, of course.'' He took a deep breath and let it out slowly. ''I don't want to live with her death on my hands. You've got to find her, Cole. Find her and tell her what's going on.''

TAYLOR CLIMBED INTO the cherry-red Explorer she'd rented from the local car dealership and backed it out of the motel parking lot. The vehicle was brand-new but she'd refused to take it until the mechanic in the back had put it up on the rack and checked everything thoroughly. Looking at her strangely, he'd pronounced the truck perfect. She turned right on Main and headed straight out of town for Diablo. She was going to finish what she'd started when the brakes had failed on the Blazer. She was going to check out the old ranch house. She needed to look around, but besides that, it'd keep her mind off Cole. She had a meeting set up with Jim Henderson for later in the day but until then she wanted something to occupy herself.

The tires hummed along the blacktop and before she knew it, she was at the cutoff. The truck bounced over the cattle guard, then she guided it carefully along the path she'd taken before. The sun was shining down and there was absolutely no possibility of bad weather. She'd even packed a lunch. Everything was taken care of and she wasn't leaving until she'd gone over every inch of the place.

She found the old house easily this time, and pumping the brakes carefully, she maneuvered down the incline toward the ruins. There was no sign of the Blazer. She'd had it towed into town before leaving so the place looked just as it had the first time she'd seen it. Fallen timbers, missing windows, open to the elements. Easing the truck into position, Taylor brought it to a stop ten or fifteen yards away from the house. She turned off the engine, then sat for a moment and looked at what was left of the former owner's home.

It had probably been a nice place when new. There was no way they could have poured a foundation on the cliff, even if they could have gotten concrete to the location, so they'd built it up on blocks instead and given it a higher elevation. A one-story home that rambled over the edge in both directions, the house had been in the shape of a U with the open area facing the view.

And what a view it was. As Taylor leaned over the steering wheel and stared into the distance, she couldn't help but compare this to the view in the window above her kitchen sink back at home. Nothing but pleasure at the sight came over her. The startling blue sky held not a single cloud, and the only point of motion for miles was a hawk riding the thermals hundreds of feet overhead. She took a cleansing breath and felt an unexpected calmness.

She opened the truck's door and slipped out, her boots touching the ground then sliding slightly on the rocky incline as she made her way toward the ruins. The air smelled sweet and clean, and its clarity seemed to bring everything closer. From the corner of her eye, a sudden movement caught her peripheral vision. She checked her breath, then let it out in relief as a mule deer flicked up his tail and bounded in the opposite direction. His crashing retreat sent up a flurry of crows from one of the piñon trees and their caws sounded loud in the cold, silent air.

At the edge of the ruins, she stopped and began to look around a little closer. The remnants of the house told the tale. The fire had obviously started in the kitchen, then worked its way to the rest of the home. The front right corner of the place was the most badly damaged, but she could still make out what had been a kitchen table and what was left of one old chair, its legs blackened and falling apart. A smut-edged pot lay beside it.

The lowest point was at the center of the house in what had been the living room. Guarding the ruins with silent stoicism, the stacked remains of the chimney and fireplace stood as a weathered reminder of what could have been. Taylor closed her eyes and imagined sitting in front of the warmth of the fireplace, snow whipping the cedars outside, wind tucking in around the eaves. She could just see Lester parking himself as close as he could to the grate, and Cole's grin as he noticed the dog. She opened her eyes abruptly. What was she doing?

Shaking her head, she moved forward, toward the stone steps that led to the fire-blackened timbers. On the left, away from the living room, had to have been the bedrooms. She walked gingerly into the center of the larger of the two rooms and stared at the eerie space.

A cedar had sprung up in one corner of the room, and the tree's limbs had spread themselves overhead to encase the area with long, brown fingers. They'd twisted and knotted themselves into the remains of the roof, and the low-hanging branches almost seemed to reach out for her. A sudden blanket of claustrophobia settled over Taylor and her breath quickened in response.

She shook her head and tried to clear the feeling. Stepping backward, she stumbled unexpectedly into the two remaining beams that marked the doorway from the bedrooms to the living room. With a wooden scream, the ancient timber gave way, and the next thing Taylor knew she was falling.

She landed with a jarring thud, pain radiating up her tailbone and down her back. For a moment, she felt faint and a dizzy black wave threatened her eyesight. She blinked away the darkness, then gingerly flexed her wrists and ankles. Nothing seemed broken, thank God. Drawing her knees to her chest, she sat still for a second and tried to calm down. As her breathing became normal again, something shiny, in the dirt and rubble, caught her eye. She never would have seen it if she hadn't fallen. She reached out but as soon as her fingers touched it, she recognized the object. Obviously new, it'd blown into the ruins and been trapped against a shattered beam. She held her breath as her fingers scratched it out of the dirt.

It was a candy wrapper. Twisted into a knot and tied.

She immediately told herself she was imagining things, but Taylor stared at the wrapper and remembered the last time she'd seen a piece of paper crimped this way. It'd been lying on Richard's desk, one of a dozen he tangled and tortured every day.

Had Richard been here? To the old ranch house?

She remembered Cole's words and the implication of what he'd learned in Houston. That Richard had been selling Jumano pottery. She'd dismissed the theory, but obviously he'd been here doing something. Her fingers tensed, the paper crackling.

Cole had found pottery shards at the cliff.

Richard had not wanted her to sell the ranch.

A sick feeling started in the pit of her stomach and made its way up her spine. Richard had come out with Jack to High Mountain that very first time and had strongly encouraged Jack to buy Diablo. She'd thought briefly of this before, but had never made the connection, never put all the pieces together. Could he have been involved in this all along?

She stood up and tried to slow her brain down. She wasn't just jumping to conclusions—she was leaping to them—and all on the basis of a tiny piece of plastic. She could only imagine what Cole would say if she showed him the wrapper and explained it all. He'd think she was the biggest nut in the world, and Shipley—oh, Lord! He'd know for sure she was loony.

Rubbing her sore butt, Taylor moved slowly to the edge of the ruins. She sat down on what was left of the ledge and stared at the tiny piece of plastic in her hand.

She was losing it, really losing it. There could be a thousand explanations, and none of them would involve Richard. He wasn't the only person in the world who tied candy wrappers into knots. He couldn't be.

A sudden noise sounded behind Taylor, a rustling and crackling sound as if someone were trampling brush and walking forward. Her heart lodging in her throat, she searched the trees and scrub, but everything was still. A nervous, slightly hysterical, giggle erupted and she couldn't hold it back. Some deer was probably standing behind the nearest cedar and having a good laugh at her expense. Turning back around, she faced the view once more.

And heard the footstep a second later, along with a whoosh of oncoming air. Ducking instantly, she got only a glimpse—a dark sweater, some kind of cap, then a swinging, blackened board. The jagged edge caught her on the side of her head and pain exploded behind her eyes.

She crumpled to the ground.

CHAPTER SIXTEEN

HE WOULDN'T BE ABLE to make it to Diablo without stopping for gas. Cursing the delay, Cole wheeled the truck into the Quik Stop and jumped outside. Inserting his credit card into the pump's slot, he pulled his coat collar up around his neck and reached for the handle, but just as the gasoline began to flow through the hose, he heard his name. He recognized the voice and turned. Beryl stood right behind him. His brain had been so occupied he hadn't even noticed her white van parked by the last pump.

Her dark eyes met his. "I need to talk to you."

"Not now," Cole answered, his voice clipped. "I've got to go out to Diablo."

"It'll only take a minute." She clasped her hands in front of her and knit her fingers together. It was an unconscious gesture of anxiety. "Please."

"Okay, but talk fast," he said. "You've got till the tank fills up."

Looking over her shoulder at the clerk who was busy behind the window, she spoke softly. "I talked to Jessica Gaskell the other day."

"Who?" The name meant nothing to Cole.

"Jessica—she's the girl who was out with Jody Jackson the night of the fall festival. I told you they came and stayed till ten, remember?''

Cole nodded.

"Jessica said Jody left in the middle of the dance and was gone for about half an hour. She'd thought he'd gone off drinking, but he didn't smell like alcohol when he came back.''

"This is old news, Beryl," he said impatiently. "I just talked to Shipley and I have a pretty good idea of what's going on. There's a guy in Houston who doesn't want Taylor out here. It's complicated and I don't have time to explain it all.''

Beryl nodded, then bit her bottom lip. He remembered her doing that, and the memory seemed to came from a different life.

"But...''

The pump clicked off. He twisted the gas cap back on, then stared at her as he returned the hose to its holder. "What?''

"Jessica said she saw Teo talking to Jody before he left, and when he came back, he went straight to Teo and they talked some more. Then...then Teo gave him some money. Jessica remembered because Jody showed it to her later. It was a hundred-dollar bill.''

Cole let the words sink in while Beryl stood beside him, looking miserable. *Teo paid Jody?*

"I think Jody tore up Taylor Matthews's motel

room." She paused. "And I think Teo paid him to do it."

"Why?" Cole spoke slowly, his hand freezing on the handle to the gasoline pump. "Why would you think that?"

She looked at him with a miserable expression. "He's been going out to Diablo, Cole. He doesn't think I know, but I followed him once. Just to the gate. I don't know what he's doing there, but I'm worried. And now there's this business... What's happening?"

Cole remembered his brother at the cave that night at Diablo. What had he been hunting? Pottery? Who better than Teo to know the most likely spots to find the rare ceramics? He'd been interested in Diablo, too. To buy it so he could mine its riches in private? And who else would have had more authority to spread the word that the ranch was haunted than the local "spirit" leader? Rumors like that would definitely keep people away and let him do his digging in private.

It all made sense.

He grabbed her arm. "Where is he? Where's Teo right now?"

"I—I don't know. He said something about going hunting early this morning..."

Cole turned around and started to get into the truck, but Beryl grabbed him. "Wait, Cole, wait!" He stopped and she spoke urgently. "If Teo's doing something he shouldn't be, please...please don't let him get hurt, Cole. Please?''

Before he could answer, she spoke again.

"I love him," she said. "Just as much as you love her."

Her words astonished him, and he stared at her in surprise, his hand on the cold metal door latch of the truck. A second later, he jerked open the door, climbed inside then started the engine with a roar.

TAYLOR OPENED HER EYES to darkness, and it took her a second to realize she was blindfolded, her hands tied behind her, her mouth gagged. It didn't take that long to understand she was in a vehicle of some sort, lying on her side. The bouncing, jostling movements and the whine of an engine told her they were going over very rough ground. She moaned as the tires hit a rut and she rolled helplessly in the opposite direction. Her head ached from the inside out, a dull, low throb that threatened her with nausea.

Who had her? Where were they taking her? What was going on?

The last thing she remembered was a glimpse of someone tall behind her. They'd swung the board without hesitation, and the instant pain against her head had been sickening. She swallowed hard and told herself to stay calm, stay focused. Surely there was a way out of this, but she wouldn't find it unless she kept her wits about her.

She had no idea how long she'd been traveling because she had no idea how long she'd been unconscious. The impression of light lingered around the edges of her blindfold, though, and she was pretty positive they were still on the ranch somewhere. The road definitely wasn't paved, that was for sure.

Another rough bump and the vehicle rocked dangerously to one side. She whimpered and rolled the other way, then just as abruptly as it'd tilted, the car stopped, sending her into a rough slide that didn't end until she hit the opposite interior wall. She swallowed her pain and strained to listen for sounds, any kind of clue as to what to expect next. She heard nothing other than a single clicking sound. When a car door opened then shut, she realized she'd heard the release of a seat belt. Only one. She tensed, but no other sounds were heard.

It seemed as though hours passed, but in reality, just a few minutes went by before the low-pitched grumble of another engine reached her ears. It sounded as if it was having trouble, and as she listened, she could hear the engine shift into another gear. A few seconds later, the crunch of rock and dirt announced the other car's arrival. The sound of the idling engine went on for a few more minutes, then surprisingly, she heard it depart, everything going deathly quiet again. Five minutes later, when she heard footsteps outside, she guessed what was going on. Obviously more than one person was involved.

They'd driven out together and one had taken her in his vehicle and the other had driven her truck. The second driver must have taken the Explorer out of sight.

A mumble of voices sounded and her mouth went dry. She couldn't be sure, but she thought only two people were talking. They came closer to where she lay. She held her breath and caught snatches of words.

"...not necessary...could have done it there."

"...more realistic...never find the body."

Taylor's spine turned into water, a column of liquid fear and disbelief. The final words were muffled, but she understood them instantly.

"...suicide...same place her husband was shot...nothing suspicious...untie her hands first... No one will ever know."

THE OLD RANCH HOUSE was abandoned, and disappointment crashed over Cole as he pulled the pickup into the empty space in front of the ruins. There was no sign of Teo's old truck, or any other vehicle for that matter. Cole opened the door of the pickup and Lester shot out to scramble into the middle of the rubble. Cole quickly followed.

He stopped just short of the steps and looked around. The fire had made a mess of everything, and time had done the rest. The fallen logs and bricks had no order left to them, no sense of what had been, except for the fireplace which was still standing.

Lester jumped over a stack of fallen debris, his toe-nails scratching against the leftover bricks.

After a few more moments of frustrated examination, Cole turned around and started back to the truck, whistling to Lester who quickly bounded out of the rubble toward him. If Teo had been here, he'd covered his tracks well, and Cole knew he could. But just then, Cole's eye caught a flattened area of grass where the weeds and dirt seemed just a little trampled, a little more level with the rocky dirt. He strode to the spot and knelt. Putting his fingers on the grass, he studied the area and let his eyes roam farther.

He saw the pattern almost immediately.

A large vehicle had been parked in the spot, and recently, too. The grass hadn't had time to spring back from the weight. Between the treads, about fifteen feet back from where they stopped, the ground was dry and dusty, a mixture of red rock and dirt. He stood up and walked slowly to the graveled area. A single footprint, way too big to be Taylor's, was barely visible in the dirt. Cole's eyes were used to picking out marks others couldn't see. Smudged and indistinct, anyone else would have missed it, but not Cole.

It was a boot print—a boot with a pointed toe and a slanted back heel. The only kind of boot Teo ever wore.

Just beside the footprint, there was another mark, longer and thinner, lasting twelve inches or more. A heavy line, drawn in the dirt with something square, something that had been dragged there.

Cole's eyes narrowed and he stood up, his curse cutting through the crisp cold air. Following the faint tire tracks, he could see where the vehicle had reversed, then turned. It had headed north.

Toward the canyon.

THE DOOR BESIDE TAYLOR swung open, and a gust of freezing wind whistled into the truck. Rough hands reached in and pulled her out, their unwelcome help necessary to keep her on her feet. As soon as she could, she jerked away from the loathsome touch, but she couldn't escape. One set of hands held her while the other pulled off her blindfold and ripped the tape from around her wrists.

She blinked in the brilliant sunlight, her eyes unable to adjust. Unbelievably, Jim Henderson stood before her. She wrenched free to look at the person behind her, and total shock rippled over her.

"Hello, Taylor." Richard smiled at her, then reached up and yanked off her gag.

Speechless, she stared at him, then back at the older man beside him. Finally she found her voice. "Wh-what's going on? What's happening?"

Both men looked at her in silence. She swung her head back toward Richard. "What are you doing here? I—I don't understand." Her voice quivered as disbelief rolled over her.

He shook his head, almost regretfully. "I told you

not to come out here, Taylor, but you just wouldn't listen, would you? If you'd stayed at home none of this would be happening. Unfortunately, now I have to take actions I wish I didn't.'' His expression tightened. ''Why didn't you just give up? Any ordinary woman would have turned and run home…the tires…your room…your brakes…''

Looking at Richard, Jim broke in. ''I told you the accident didn't rattle her. Did you think I was lying?''

Flabbergasted, Taylor stared at the real estate agent. ''Th-that was you? You did all that?''

''Let's just say I arranged the details.''

She stared at him, then without any warning, her conversation came back, the one she'd had with him right after her brakes went out. With startling clarity, she remembered her unexplained anxiety, and now she realized why she'd felt that way. His words rang in her mind. *''You're very lucky the brakes didn't go out when you were nearer the edge.''* Cole had never told Jim about her brakes. He'd merely said she'd had a car accident. She'd sensed, almost subconsciously, something was off with the conversation but at the time she hadn't been able to figure it out.

Now she knew.

All she could do was gape at him. ''W-what about the client…was he fake, too?''

Jim grinned. ''No, sweetheart. He was real—just like the shots I had Jody fire over our heads that day.'' He spoke in a high, mocking voice. '''I'm so sorry, Taylor, but I can't risk bringing any more clients out here…' Hell, I never expected anyone to actually call about the damned ad. Shocked the hell out of me when that kid phoned. I had to do something to scare him off.''

"To scare him off…" Taylor stared at Jim a second longer, then she turned slowly to Richard, the truth dawning on her. "You're selling pottery you've found here, aren't you?"

"You always were smart, Taylor. But you let your emotions take over this time. You didn't think about it or you would have figured it out, I'm sure."

The sickening realization of what the truth really meant came over her. "How long have you been…" She stopped, her throat too tight to continue.

"Long enough to make a substantial amount," Richard said, "but not long enough to quit. That's why I couldn't let you sell the ranch."

Taylor's eyes went to Jim's. "And you were in on this? Why?"

His face tightened, a look of controlled anger passing over his expression. "I used to make a damned good living out here. Selling ranches and farms. Then the market fell apart. What was I supposed to do? How was I supposed to live?"

She closed her eyes, saw his office with the expensive rug, the outdated furniture—once nice but now threadbare.

Opening her eyes, she swung her gaze back to

Richard. Her voice was a whisper. "How could you do this? I...I thought I knew you..."

Something flickered in his eyes. It resembled regret, but she couldn't tell for sure. He moved closer and took her chin between his fingers. "You weren't supposed to be part of all this, Taylor. It was supposed to be clean, taken care of with one accident, but you had the bad luck to be wounded when Jack was killed. The plans had to be changed."

"*'When Jack was killed?'*" The words came out hoarsely, then understanding came in a blinding flash. "Are you...are you telling me you had Jack murdered?"

"Yes. I arranged it all."

She groaned, then staggered, the words a physical blow. She thought she would throw up, then she managed to gather some control, to draw a breath from lungs that had suddenly stopped working. "Why..."

"I didn't need him anymore. Once I'd convinced him to buy Diablo, keeping him around was pointless. He'd gotten too conservative. If he didn't want me to buy the kinds of pieces I had in the past, I knew he'd never go for selling pottery that hadn't been approved. He had no vision, no idea of the money we could make."

Taylor's throat closed, fingers of disbelief choking off her air. She struggled to find the words. "You killed him for that?"

Richard shrugged. "It was his fault, Taylor. He could have gone along with me."

Taylor stared at him, then stumbled backward and lost her balance. She tumbled down, into the dirt. He looked down at her.

"You could have stayed out of all this, Taylor. If you'd been content to stay home, you wouldn't be in the predicament you're in now. Everything would have been just fine. I told you not to sell the ranch, but you wouldn't listen and this is where we've ended up."

Jim's voice interrupted the tirade. "We need to take care of business, Richard. I don't like standing out here in the open. We can be seen for miles."

For the first time, Taylor looked around and realized where she was. They were close to the canyon. Just over the next rise, the cliffs waited. Her heart clutched suddenly and she understood the conversation she'd heard before, the image of their endless height bringing another sweep of fear with it. She scrambled to her feet, her eyes darting over the nearby landscape for any possible escape route.

Richard looked at Jim and spoke. "You got the gun?"

"It's in the Rover."

"Go get it."

She stared at Richard and he stared at her. Finally he turned her around roughly and pushed her ahead of him, forcing her to walk in front of him. When they got over the ridge, the canyon stretched out in front of them, ten yards of scrub and rocky soil between them and the terrifying edge.

"You can't do this," she said, stumbling to a stop.

"Of course I can," he answered. "It's the perfect crime."

"Shipley will know."

"Shipley wouldn't know a crime if it jumped up and bit him on the butt. He's an incompetent idiot with an overblown sense of his own importance."

"Maybe," she answered, "but Cole isn't. He'll figure it out, if he hasn't already."

"You're right," Richard answered. "In fact, I'm sure Mr. Reynolds will be here soon and we'll take care of him, too."

Taylor's heart froze as she took in his meaning. "Y-you're not thinking straight, Richard." She tried to keep her voice level and calm, tried to hide the panic rising inside her as a wave from a storm. "You'll be the only one left at Williams/Matthews. You'll be under suspicion eventually even if they think my death is a suicide."

"I don't think so. You were just too despondent and never recovered from Jack's death. Dr. Kornfeld can testify to that. And that pitiful journal you've been keeping on the computer at work will show your state of mind if no one believes her."

"Journal!"

He smiled gently, an expression that chilled her more than anything had so far.

She got desperate. "But if you shoot me, they'll know it wasn't suicide."

"Not if your fingerprints are on the trigger."

A sick feeling washed over her. "What is it you want, Richard? I—I'll do it, whatever it is. Just tell me."

"Don't beg, Taylor."

She licked her lips. "I—I'm not begging. I'm making you an offer, a business offer. You just tell me what it is you want out of this deal, and I'll give it to you. Money? The company? The ranch? Tell me."

His eyes narrowed and he took a step toward her. "No amount of money would buy your way out of this. I have a very lucrative underground business going and my reputation depends on it. There's nothing you could give me to replace that." He paused. "I told you you were making a mistake, Taylor, but you wouldn't listen. I'm not the kind of person you can just use then toss aside when you're finished. I listened to you cry after Jack's death, and I was always there for you. Always. Then when you fell in love with Reynolds, you weren't interested in me anymore."

"He wasn't the reason—"

"Don't lie to me. Not now. When you came into the gallery and broke it off with me, I knew the truth. I knew it, but I chose to ignore it, that's all. But I'm not ignoring it now."

"You've got it all wrong—"

"I don't think so. I went by your house the next day and I saw him leave then come back…with your breakfast. Friends don't do that, Taylor. Just lovers."

"You don't know what you're talking about. Cole and I weren't—"

She stopped talking when Jim walked up, a rifle in his hand. He thrust it in Richard's direction. "Here you go," he said.

Richard looked down at the gun, then back up at Jim. "This is your job, remember?" he said coldly. "We divided the labor a long time ago. *You* do the dirty work—I sell the pottery."

"I did the last one." Jim's tone was totally unfeeling, as if they were discussing something other than Taylor's very life. "I think it's time you make the same kind of commitment to this little project that I have."

Richard glanced at Taylor, then jerked his gaze back to Jim. "Just do it," he growled. "Do it or I'll see both of you fall off that cliff."

The older man's expression shifted, and Taylor's heart lurched to a stop. She had to do something— anything… She threw herself toward Richard and grabbed him around the shoulders, pinning his arms. It was a deadly embrace. To shoot her, Jim would have to shoot Richard, too.

As Richard squirmed to get away from her, Jim lowered the gun and ordered her to stop. She ignored both of them, her heart in her throat as she struggled against Richard's firm weight. He was in excellent shape; she knew she could only hold out for so long. If he forced her arms away, it'd be over and fast.

She held on for her life and they shuffled in the dirt, puffs of dust rising around them, Jim still yelling. She aimed for Richard's eyes, but her nails missed and trailed down his cheek. He screamed, but managed to get the upper hand. Grabbing her arms, he freed himself, both of them glaring at each other, their chests rising and falling from the encounter. She jerked away but he cursed and pulled her tight to keep his grip.

Breathing heavily, Taylor flung her hair from her face. Then her eyes widened as she realized what he'd done. While they'd been fighting, he'd managed to drag her all the way to the edge of the canyon. They were standing on the precipice, tottering really, right on the edge. Dizzy and sick with fear, she looked at him.

He smiled at her.

And then he pushed.

CHAPTER SEVENTEEN

COLE'S TRUCK TOPPED the ridge to the west of the old ranch house, and he immediately saw the bright red Explorer. He didn't recognize the vehicle so he cut off his own engine and parked where he was. Grabbing his rifle, he told the dog to stay, then jumped out and headed toward the truck.

It was empty with no sign of anyone else around. Looking through the window, he saw the doors were unlocked so he opened one. A small lunch sack and a thermos rested on the seat, and beside them was a purse. A black leather bag that looked a lot like the one he'd seen draped over Taylor's shoulder when she'd climbed out of his own truck two days before. His throat closed up.

He quietly pushed in the door but didn't close it completely. His arrival didn't need to be announced until he knew what in the hell was happening. He headed straight for the bluff in front of him, and beyond it, Diablo Canyon.

He reached the top within seconds. Then time stopped and so did his heart.

TAYLOR TOTTERED ON THE edge. Then she screamed and reached out, her hands grabbing only air.

Richard's eyes glittered as he jumped back to avoid her but she snatched again, and this time, she managed to grab the edge of his sweater with both hands. The crumbling edge gave way, and Richard fell to his knees, Taylor clinging to him. Her eyes searched behind him to plead with Jim for help, but he'd disappeared.

Her cries echoed back and forth along the canyon walls. "Richard! Please! Please, don't do this."

He was forcing her fingers from his sweater, bending them backward.

With her legs over the edge, Taylor fought for a hold but her boots scrabbled uselessly against the rocky side of the cliff. She screamed and dug her fingers into the dirt, her other hand still clutching Richard's sweater.

Richard cursed roundly just as she crammed her knee into the rocky soil, and her foot found the smallest toehold. Using the minute leverage, she grunted and got her fingers around Richard's wrist, but he twisted quickly and slipped his shoulders out of the sweater. Taylor cried out as she slid another few inches. She had a slim purchase in the dirt but the only thing really keeping her from falling was the sleeve where the wool had inadvertently trapped itself around Richard's wrist and her own—a lifeline of threads.

And that's when she saw Cole.

He held a gun at hip height as he strode across

the bluff, his black leather coat flaring out with each step. He was her savior, her future, the life she had left. She cried out his name, and Richard turned.

"Go ahead and shoot," he screamed. "Shoot, then we'll both go over the edge."

Cole stopped twelve feet away. His face was a mask of anger. "Bring her up. Right now."

Richard shook his head. "You put down the gun. Then I'll bring her up."

Cole flicked his eyes in Taylor's direction. If he shot Richard, she'd go over for sure. If Cole put down his gun, Richard could still shove her away. Either way it was a gamble—a gamble with her life.

With his eyes on Richard's, Cole slowly bent his knees and laid the rifle on the ground. He eased back up and held his hands out in front of him. "All right. I'm not armed. We can end this thing right now with no one getting hurt." He glanced toward Taylor, his dark eyes full of emotion, then he focused on Richard once more. "Pull her up and step away from the edge."

She looked at Richard and he met her gaze, then both of them looked at the sweater. It was navy cashmere, she noticed for the first time, and the herringbone pattern waved dizzily as she stared at it. Richard's fingers were wrapped around the shoulder and she held on to the sleeve.

Taylor swallowed hard, then her heart stood still. One by one, his fingers opened and the wool slipped through them.

She screamed Cole's name as she pitched backward.

COLE LAUNCHED HIMSELF in Taylor's direction, but Richard stepped in front of him and grabbed both his arms to stop him. Cole struggled to get out of the other man's grip but he had surprising strength. They scuffled in the dirt, their grunts of effort and curses echoing through the canyon. Richard swung at Cole's jaw, but Cole managed to dodge the blow. He was taller and younger but Richard was strong and desperate. He swung again and connected but Cole answered with a punch of his own, and Richard went down.

But only for a second. He scrambled sideways and headed for the rifle he'd forced Cole to abandon. Torn between looking over the edge for Taylor and dealing with Richard, Cole had little choice. He swung around in time to see Richard raise the gun to his shoulder and take aim. Cole threw himself forward, his hands on the barrel, the gun between them.

They struggled over the weapon, their shuffling feet kicking up dirt. Cole forced Richard backward, but the older man fought hard. By the time Cole got control, they were at the very edge of the bluff, Richard on his knees, Cole towering above him.

''Turn loose,'' Cole growled. ''Turn loose of the gun, and get up.''

Richard's eyes met Cole's. Instead of answering,

he pushed back unexpectedly and managed to get his finger on the trigger. Their eyes met over the barrel.

Cole had no choice. He put his hands on the rifle, yanked it up then pushed. The gun discharged into the air with a thundering report and losing his balance, Richard began to tumble off the edge.

For just one second, their eyes met and held. Then Richard windmilled his arms and disappeared from Cole's vision, falling over the cliff.

His cries rang out all the way down.

Cole stumbled to the edge, his heart refusing to beat until he spotted Taylor. She was sprawled on a tiny ledge, a few feet from where she'd fallen, a small, still figure. He called her name, but she didn't move. Easing himself over, he ignored the drop, the wind, and everything else, but Taylor.

TAYLOR'S EYES FLUTTERED open as a stabbing, uncontrollable pain shot down her arm and into her shoulder. Cole's dark eyes looked into her own with anxiousness. "Hold on, Taylor. We're almost to the truck, just a few more feet. I think you've got some broken ribs and a dislocated shoulder, but I'll get you out of here in no time. Just hold on." She was in his arms and even though he was being as careful as he could, each step he took brought with it a stab of red-hot agony.

She licked her lips and tried to speak. The effort

seemed gargantuan but she struggled to form the words, knowing she had to.

"Be quiet," he said. "It's over."

"No…" The words came out in husky croak just as they reached the truck. "Not over."

"He's gone, Taylor. I promise you. Richard's—"

"He wasn't a-alone."

Cole's arms tightened around her and before she could speak, he answered her. "I know," he said grimly. "Teo's involved in this, isn't he? Where is he? Have you seen him?"

She shook her head. "N-no. Not Teo…Jim…Jim Henderson…" Her voice died out as a sweep of blackness came over her.

Cole spoke with sudden urgency. "*What?* Are you saying Jim Henderson was involved? Not Teo?"

"Yes. He…was with Richard. He…he was the one who was helping. He was here but he ran off…"

Cole jerked his eyes up just as she spoke, and like an apparition she'd managed to conjure, Jim was standing in front of them, a rifle in his hands.

"Put her in the truck." The older man's words were measured and even. He opened the door and stepped to one side. "Now."

Cole gently laid Taylor on the seat. She groaned and curled into herself, but her gaze stayed on Jim and didn't waver.

"Step away from the truck." Jim pointed with the

rifle to a spot between Taylor and himself. "Over there."

Cole moved slowly, Jim circling him. They stopped with Jim to one side, and Cole facing Taylor, his hands held out, an outcropping of rocks setting the stage behind the two men. "You can't get away with this, Jim. There's a body at the bottom of Diablo. It'll all come out."

"That body's not the first. It won't be the last."

Taylor listened to the exchange, a firelike pain shooting down her shoulder. She grabbed her arm and held on. She had to do something, but what? Suddenly, a hint of movement from a rock behind Cole caught her eye. She gasped just as Teo raised a rifle and rested it on the granite in front of him.

At the sound, both of the men turned.

And time stopped.

Taylor's eyes never left Cole's face. It drained completely of color when he saw his brother. A second later, Teo's rifle went off.

And Jim Henderson fell to the dirt.

SNOW WAS DRIFTING DOWN when Taylor and Cole walked out of the sheriff's office that evening. Without saying a word, they went to Cole's pickup and climbed inside. Cole marveled that Taylor could move as well as she could. With her arm in a sling, and her ribs taped, she wore three butterfly bandages and a bruise the size of an orange.

But she'd never looked more beautiful.

She settled into the seat, a stiff air to her posture that spoke of the wrapped and hurting ribs beneath her sweater. Feeling his gaze, she looked up at him.

Their stare connected across the seat, then suddenly she was in his arms and crying. Cole patted her awkwardly, trying not to cause her any more pain than she was already feeling, but wanting to comfort her as well. She lifted her face to his and their lips found each other's. The kiss held comfort and love and everything else Cole knew had been missing from his life.

And would stay missing, too.

He put his hands on her shoulders and gently pulled back. Her eyes glittered in the darkness, then reading something in his own expression, something he wished wasn't there, she blinked and drew away—drew away just as he'd wanted.

She was beautiful and smart and brave and just looking at her made him ache. But there had never been a chance of a future for them and any hope otherwise, which might have once existed, had now been destroyed.

Taylor would never be able to look at Cole without thinking of Teo. The two brothers were linked— by birth and now by death.

She looked at him in the dark. "It's over, isn't it? Us, I mean?"

Cole stared at her. He couldn't explain his feelings. They were a strange mixture of shame, embarrassment and grief. "There isn't an us. There never was."

She shook her head, a miserable expression on her face. "But there could be."

"Not now." His voice was gentle. "My brother started all this, Taylor. He's the reason Jack was killed even if he didn't pull the trigger. You could never live with me, knowing that."

"Teo has nothing to do with us. This is between you and me."

"You say that now, but once you think about it, you'll feel differently. Besides, you knew from the very beginning it wouldn't work, Taylor. There's more than just Teo between us. You hate it out here—and here is where I belong."

"But I didn't mean it," she cried. "It was just something to say—"

"It was the truth." He put his hand against her face, her skin so incredibly soft. "And even if it wasn't, it wouldn't matter. West Texans are different... We don't think—or act—like other people. I could never live anywhere else, Taylor. You can head back to Houston now. You've got a business to run. And I've got my life here."

She twisted her face to put her lips against his hand. He closed his eyes and listened to the sound of his heart breaking. When she faced him again, her eyes held tears. "Is it Beryl? Do you still love her?"

He answered without thinking. "She's got nothing to do with this. Nothing."

"Then what? I need to know what's keeping us apart, Cole, because I love you," she said. "I really do love you."

"I love you, too. But it'd never work. Not in a million years." His words sounded empty, even to his ears.

"That's not answering my question." Her expression turned fierce. "You just don't want to try, do you? You're too scared to try."

"Don't be ridiculous."

Her eyes filled up, then overflowed. "I know what I'm talking about, Cole. Believe me. When I saw Jim holding that gun on you, I thought I was going to die. And all I could do was think about what a mistake I'd made—"

"It *was* a mistake."

She shook her head. "Not the kind you mean. I'm talking about a mistake of my own. I'd been too scared to admit how much I really loved you because I was afraid of being hurt again. I was holding back just to protect myself. Then I realized I was facing my biggest fear, right then and there."

"A gun in Jim's hands?"

"A gun pointed at you." She took a deep breath. "It was the past all over again. The man I cared about in danger once more. And I realized I was going to lose everything—lose it without ever even having it."

He shook his head. "This isn't the same thing, Taylor."

"It is. You're too scared to love me and you can't even admit it. You're just using Teo as an excuse...just as I've used my emotions in the past. Needing closure before I could commit to Richard, then using my fear before giving in to my love for you."

He stared at her from across the seat, the lights outside the foggy window of the parked truck indistinct blurs of movement and life. Where they sat, time had stopped. It was jarring to realize it was continuing outside.

"You don't understand," he said quietly.

She spoke, her voice low and suddenly hard. "I do understand, Cole. I understand too well...and that's the problem." She turned and looked out the windshield. Her profile was carved ivory perfection as she pulled her coat closer to her. "Take me to my motel, please. I'd like to pack and get out of here."

THE CONDO WAS MUSTY and stale when Taylor walked inside. She nodded toward the wall of the marble foyer. "You can put the bags there." Digging some bills out of her wallet, she paid the cabbie, then shut the door behind him and leaned against it, closing her eyes.

The trip had been a nightmare, every movement agony, every thought a painful one. She didn't know what hurt more—her ribs or her heart. Both felt as though they'd been removed, broken in two, and stuffed back in without direction.

Sighing deeply, she opened her eyes and walked into the darkened kitchen. There was nothing in the refrigerator, she knew, but she opened it anyway and stared at the empty shelves. Standing there, with the pale, dim light of the open appliance throwing shadows across the room, she looked up and her eyes filled with tears. On the cabinet, in a bud vase, was the single red rose—dead now—that Cole had brought her the morning after they'd made love.

She closed the refrigerator, walked across the room and sat down at the kitchen table. Very slowly, very carefully, she laid her head on the wooden top and began to cry.

CHAPTER EIGHTEEN

THE AIR WAS SO HEAVY and cold Cole could almost taste it. Diego snorted and tossed his head, a plume of white steam coming from each side of the horse's nose. Cole patted the animal with his gloved hand and murmured some meaningless words while his eyes studied the land stretching out in front of him for signs of white-tailed deer. He didn't see anything, but then again, he wasn't really trying. He'd come out to Diablo to search his soul, not look for game. It was habit, pure and simple, that made him scan the terrain.

He nudged the horse into movement and they started forward. Lester, content to be along, trotted nearby, ranging behind and then in front of them to occasionally investigate something interesting. Thorny bushes pulled at them right and left, but neither man nor animals seemed to notice. And it'd been that way, at least for Cole, for the past five days. He'd headed straight for the ranch shortly after Taylor had left High Mountain. If he'd thought about it, it might have seemed strange to him—to go right back to the place where so much tragedy had occurred. Then again...maybe it was the only place he *could* have gone.

Diego picked his way without guidance from the man on his back, and much later, Cole found himself in a part of the ranch he hadn't been to in a very long time. The springs.

Lester splashed into the edge of the water as Cole slid off the horse, pulling his saddlebags with him and wondering if Taylor even knew about the spot. More likely than not, she didn't. To Cole's way of thinking, this was the best place on the spread. He'd never seen an Arabian oasis, but he was sure even those fabled havens weren't as beautiful or as peaceful as this.

A circle of trees guarded the spring itself. Mostly cedars and mesquites on the fringes, a lone cypress waited nearest the water. The graceful branches of the tree reached toward the spring like a woman bending over, and the water bubbled up continually as if it were trying to touch her. There were always birds here—cardinals, blue jays, crows. As Cole walked up, a mockingbird cried out from an overhead branch, the sound as shrill and startling as a baby's cry.

Ignoring the bird and his master as well, Diego wandered away and began to munch at the abundant native grass. After drinking his fill of the clear, cold water, Lester flopped down and promptly went to sleep, clearly exhausted. Cole sat down in the quiet, still coldness and watched the sun pull a blanket of stars behind it as it slipped slowly toward the horizon.

What had he done?

What in the hell had he done?

With a movement of infinite weariness, he brought his hands up to his face and rubbed them over his eyes and cheeks. Five days of stubble wasn't stubble anymore—it'd gone straight to beard. He didn't require a mirror to know he looked like shit. He felt like it, too.

He dropped his hands and gazed into the darkness. Somewhere over the next ridge he could hear a javelina and behind him, Diego stopped to listen, too, Lester's ears twitching as he continued to sleep.

Taylor had told him he was afraid to love and Cole had told her she was wrong. But the more he thought about her parting words, the sharper they dug into his mind. Like the barbed wire stretching for miles around Diablo, her accusations refused to let him get away. Her words mingled with the conversation he'd had with Teo. Cole had stopped at his brother's house on the way to Diablo. It was the first time, in a very long time, that Cole had stepped into the small, white-frame home.

He'd had no real reason to be there—at least not one he could have admitted to. A few hours later, when he'd left, Cole had understood.

The same thing that had brought Taylor back to Diablo had taken Cole to Teo's house. He hadn't known what would occur when he got there, and

even now, thinking back to it, he wasn't sure what
had happened or where he stood with his brother.
He had a feeling things would never be completely
resolved between him and Teo no matter how much
they talked. Yet their relationship wasn't one that
could be put in a box and labeled "finished." It was
too complicated for that and always would be.

Teo had opened the screen door and stood motionless behind it for so long, Cole hadn't thought
he was going to let him in. After several moments,
he had finally stepped aside. Removing his hat, Cole
had entered the small, dark living room. The two
brothers stared at each other then Cole broke the
awkward silence. "I came to say thank you. You
saved my life out at Diablo."

Teo's dark eyes were impossible to read. "You're
welcome, baby brother. I'm sure you would have
done the same for me."

"Why'd you do it, Teo? What were you doing
with Henderson and Williams?"

Teo stayed silent long enough to make Cole uncomfortable before he began to explain. Finding the
first pot at Diablo. Approaching Richard and telling
him about it. Offering to sell him more, then refusing to continue when Richard had tried to get him
to kill Jack.

"I knew you'd never believe I had nothing to do
with the killing. You always did think the worst of
me. That's why I didn't try to explain before." Teo
shook his head. "The truth is the people need me,

Cole, and need the things I can get for them. Computers for the kids, heaters for the old folks... No one cares anymore but me. I had to have money for those things, so I sold Richard the first pot. When I found out he wanted Jack killed, I got out.''

''Just like that?'' Cole didn't bother to hide his skepticism. ''Williams would never have let you walk away—''

''He didn't have a choice.'' Teo's voice was cold and blunt. ''I'd recorded all our conversations plus I got a buddy to catch us with his camcorder. I put the tapes in a safety deposit box with instructions for J. C. Shipley. If anything had happened to me, Williams would have had a lot of tough questions to face.'' Teo paused. ''It's one thing to arrange the murder of a stranger out here—it's a whole different thing to kill the head of the local Indian Council. Williams was smart enough to see the difference. The uproar would have ruined his little scheme completely.''

Teo paused then took a deep breath. ''I been trying to figure out ever since who took my place. I knew Williams had to have a local helping him. I'd stay at the ranch, look for clues. I spread the rumors about ghosts to keep people away. I even paid Jody Jackson to snoop around and tell me if he heard any rumors.'' He shook his head. ''Obviously I trusted the wrong kid. I never would have thought it was Henderson...and that he was paying Jody, too.''

Cole stood mute. There was nothing else he could do.

Teo said the words for him. "You assumed it was me, didn't you? Helping Williams?" He paused and looked directly into Cole's eyes. "I've never been the bad guy you thought I was, little brother."

"It's more than that—"

"I know, I know. You had good reason. There's a lot between us, not the least of which is the fact that I took your woman. Any man would have done the same." Teo's stare seemed to go through Cole, to pass the skin and muscle and blood, and go straight into his heart. "I didn't steal her, though, Cole. It wasn't like that at all. It wasn't...planned. We just fell in love."

A long, narrow patch of sunlight snuck into the room. It hit the small, braided rug on the floor, then slanted into the blue chair beside the window. Cole sat down abruptly on the sofa opposite the chair. Teo sat down, too, the springs creaking against his weight.

"Tell me what happened." Cole's voice was husky, hard to understand. "Exactly what happened."

"After you left, she kept coming by the house. You never wrote her and she didn't know where you were, what you were doing. She thought maybe we were getting letters and would know more about what was happening with you." Teo held out his hands. "We didn't know anything, of course, but she kept showing up. Every week she'd stop. One day I offered to take her to the post office so we could both check. When we left there, we went and got a cup of coffee and I listened to her.'' Teo lifted his eyes to Cole's and again, the strange sensation came over him...of his gaze going directly inside him. ''I listened to her cry because you were gone. Every week she came by and every week I would listen. One night, she said 'thank you,' and then she kissed me. The next week, when she did the same thing, the kiss turned into something else. Before we knew it, we were in love.''

''Just like that?''

Teo looked at him impassively, then finally he spoke. ''I guess I should have pushed her away, but I didn't. I couldn't.''

''Why didn't she ever explain...''

''If she had tried to tell you, you wouldn't have believed her. Your ears were closed to the truth, your eyes blind. Even when we were kids, once you made up your mind you never saw anything else.''

Turning his head, Cole stared out the window beside the chair where he sat. A single mesquite tree stood near the edge of the fence line. It seemed to shiver in the wind. ''All I had to go on was the past.'' He turned back to face his brother. ''It wouldn't have been the first time you took what you wanted.''

''That's what you think, but you always seem to forget one thing—in High Mountain, if your skin's too dark, you take what you want fast or you don't get it at all. Mother taught us that.''

Cole's lips tightened. ''Maybe she taught you that. My lesson was slightly different.''

''And you don't even know why, do you?'' For the first time, Teo's voice softened. ''You never understood, did you?''

When Cole didn't answer, Teo spoke again. ''Every time she looked at you, she saw your father—''

Cole spoke in sudden fury. ''Don't you think I know that? She hated his guts and mine, too. It was more than clear how she felt about him, but I paid the price.''

Teo shook his head. ''You've got it all wrong.''

''I wasn't that blind or deaf, Teo. Don't try and tell me—''

''Your father was the only man she ever loved— really loved—and he left her. When she saw you, all she saw was her biggest disappointment—that he'd left her. It wasn't personal.''

Stunned, Cole stared at Teo, his mouth going dry. ''You're crazy,'' he finally managed to say.

''No, I'm not. Mother and I talked about it, just before she died. She felt bad because she'd never explained it to you, but she said every time she thought about trying, she knew it wouldn't matter. You wouldn't have listened.''

''She should have tried.''

"You're right. She was wrong not to talk to you about it...but she did the best she could."

The look they shared was long and measured. It held memories and old hurts and the shimmer of regret. But the past was the past. They were grown men and how they handled their relationship now depended on them and no one else.

There was nothing left to say after that.

Cole picked up his hat from the nearby table. Crushing the brim between his fingers, he sat silently a second more, then he stood. Teo rose from his own chair, and they faced each other in the tiny room. The moment was awkward and agonizing, and Cole didn't know what to do. There *might* come a time when he was ready to forget and forgive...but it wasn't now.

Sensing Cole's emotions, Teo simply nodded once, his eyes as hooded and dark as always. Cole left then, his boots ringing on the porch.

Alone in the cold, dark night, remembering the conversation, Cole kept thinking of the look of love in Beryl's eyes when she'd asked him to keep Teo safe. How could Cole have been so blind all these years? She'd always loved Teo, obviously loved him more than she'd loved Cole, and he'd never fully understood. It'd been easier to blame his brother, to blame him for everything, but now, after thinking some more about their conversation, Cole knew the truth.

If he had truly loved Beryl—as she loved Teo—

then nothing would have kept Cole from her. But it hadn't been true love. Infatuation, lust, affection...anything, but not love.

Not the way Beryl loved Teo.

Not the way Taylor loved Cole.

Every word Taylor had spoken had been right on the money. He'd never taken a chance, never let himself even try to love again after Beryl had gone to Teo. All these years, without even understanding what he was doing, Cole had used his past as an excuse not to get close to anyone, just as Taylor had said. All those clichéd arguments he'd given Taylor about them being from two different worlds had meant nothing.

Real love waited. Real love was always there whether or not the person was, too. His mother had proved that, hadn't she? In a negative way. Taylor was the perfect example of the right way, though. She loved Cole, and she'd never hold Teo's actions against Cole. Taylor wasn't that kind of woman— she hadn't come to High Mountain for revenge. She'd come for justice, and that had definitely been served.

Cole slept better that night than he had in weeks, and when dawn broke, he headed straight for home. He was in Houston by sunset.

THE DOORBELL CHIMED softly but Taylor jerked as if an alarm had gone off right in her ear. She wasn't expecting a soul—in fact, only Martha knew she'd come back from High Mountain. The solitude had been planned—she'd been hiding out for a week, unable to bring herself to go to the office and face all the explanations—but she hadn't been prepared for the overwhelming feeling of despair that had come with it. Taylor slipped on her house shoes and made her way to the front door. Standing on her tiptoes, she looked through the peephole and her breath caught in her chest. Cole! She sent a wild glance into the mirror by the front door and cursed, but there was nothing she could do about her hair or makeup. All she could do was open the door.

He stood on the threshold for what seemed like forever, then he opened his arms and moved toward her, his coat flapping wide and embracing her just as he did. Their lips met and Taylor felt as though a missing part of her had been found.

They held each other forever, then Taylor pulled back and looked up at Cole. "Would you like to come in?" she asked idiotically.

He grinned. "Yeah—I think I'd like that a lot..."

He stepped inside the house, and replaced the emptiness with his presence, the loneliness with warmth. "I missed you," he said. Taking off his coat, he turned to her and held out his arms again. Without a second's hesitation, she moved into his embrace. "I feel like the biggest fool in the world for letting you leave High Mountain. I can't believe I did it. I love you, Taylor. Love you with everything I've got inside me. Can you forgive me for being so dense?''

Taylor's heart flipped over inside her chest and a feeling she never expected to experience again threatened to overcome her. Happiness. "I think I can manage that," she answered.

"Are you sure? After everything that happened?"

"Oh, Cole, you weren't responsible for any of that, and you know it." Her hands locked around his neck. "We're okay and that's the main thing, right? It's over. Done with. I never blamed Teo."

"I know. And I shouldn't have, either. We had a long talk, Teo and I, before I came here."

A light came into her eyes, the green depths taking on a loving look. "You reconciled?"

"Let's just say he explained some things to me, and I understand the situation better now. He was still involved in the whole mess, though. Can you live with that?"

She leaned back, still in the circle of his arms. "I went to High Mountain to find out the truth and that's what I did. It was the uncertainty I couldn't live with—not the truth. What about you? Can you handle it?"

"As long as I have you." His arms tightened around her. "Do I? Do I have you, Taylor?"

She reached up and kissed him deeply. When they parted there were tears shimmering in her eyes. "You'll always have me, Cole...for as long as you want me. That's what life is about. You can't go around hiding because you're afraid something bad is going to happen. You just have to live. All the time. Live and love.''

Cole nodded slowly. "You're a very wise woman, you know that?''

She laughed and shook her head, but he spoke again before she could deny it.

"It's one of the things I love about you, but I have a million other reasons I'll tell you about another day.'' He pulled her closer, his hands warm against her back, his loving embrace her every dream. "Right now, we're going to catch up then we'll plan the rest of our lives together tomorrow. How does that sound?''

"I think it sounds terrific.'' She grinned. "But there's one thing we have to get straight right now, and that's what to do about Diablo.''

"We'll do whatever you want to do with it. You decide.''

"I already have.''

He raised one eyebrow. "You're a fast worker, aren't you?''

"Well, you know that old ranch house? How good are you with a saw and hammer? It's got such a terrific view…''

His mouth actually fell open. "You'd really want to live at the ranch?''

"I can't think of any place I'd rather be.'' Her eyes pierced his. "I want to wake up every morning with you beside me and that terrific view outside.''

He nodded slowly, thoughtfully. "Well, Taylor, that's fine, but you know, life—"

"—is different out in West Texas," she finished with a smile. "I know. That's what I'm counting on. I want it to be different and I want it to be with you. Forever and ever."

He leaned down and kissed her, his soft Texas twang warming her ear. "Forever's just about long enough for me."

Heart of the West

A brand-new Harlequin continuity series
begins in July 1999
with

Husband for Hire
by
Susan Wiggs

*Beautician Twyla McCabe was Dear Abby
with a blow-dryer, listening to everyone else's
troubles. But now her well-meaning customers
have gone too far. No way was she attending
the Hell Creek High School Reunion with Rob
Carter, M.D. Who would believe a woman
who dyed hair for a living could be engaged
to such a hunk?*

Here's a preview!

CHAPTER ONE

"This isn't for the masquerade. This is for me."

"What's for you?"

"This."

Rob didn't move fast, but with a straightforward deliberation she found oddly thrilling. He gripped Twyla by the upper arms and pulled her to him, covering her mouth with his.

Dear God, a kiss. She couldn't remember the last time a man had kissed her. And what a kiss. It was everything a kiss should be—sweet, flavored with strawberries and wine and driven by an underlying passion that she felt surging up through him, creating an answering need in her. She rested her hands on his shoulders and let her mouth soften, open. He felt wonderful beneath her hands, his muscles firm, his skin warm, his mouth... She just wanted to drown in him, drown in the passion. If he was faking his ardor, he was damned good. When he stopped kissing her, she stepped back. Her disbelieving fingers went to her mouth, lightly touching her moist, swollen lips.

"That...wasn't in the notes," she objected weakly.

"I like to ad–lib every once in a while."

"I need to sit down." Walking backward, never taking her eyes off him, she groped behind her and found the Adirondack-style porch swing. *Get a grip,* she told herself. *It was only a kiss.*

"I think," he said mildly, "it's time you told me just why you were so reluctant to come back here for the reunion."

"And why I had to bring a fake fiancé as a shield?"

Very casually, he draped his arm along the back of the porch swing. "I'm all ears, Twyla. Why'd I have to practically hog–tie you to get you back here?"